PURE
By
KIM ALEXANDER

ISBN 9798201286026

Edited by Carly Hayward of Book Light Editorial

Cover Art by Pretty AF Designs
Formatted for print by Pretty A.F. Designs

Dedication

For Dyon, my own personal unicorn.

Pure

1

he unicorn walked right past me.

Maybe it didn't notice me because I was standing behind my car. I know, a Mini Cooper isn't that big, and I was just standing there with my key in my hand and my mouth hanging open. But it didn't look my way; it just kept walking up the middle of Kenyon Street like it was an enchanted grove or something. It was getting close to 4:30 in the morning, so there wasn't any traffic, just some late night drinkers looking for Ubers, and me, getting off my bartending shift at the Hare. I had to park two blocks away as usual, and I just stood there, watching as it went by. At the moment I was alone on the street, so no one else saw it. I couldn't move. I couldn't breathe. I didn't even think to take a picture.

When it was about a half a block ahead of me, I quietly stashed my purse under my car, hunched over and followed it, hiding myself on the other side of the line of parked cars. I didn't want to startle it, I guess. I looked up the street, and saw where it was going. Another block up, lit up by a streetlight, a girl stood in the middle of the road. She was slight, wearing skinny jeans and a gauzy blouse, and she looked young. She had a lot of blonde hair, and she had her hand held out, and the unicorn went straight to her. It stood in front of her and lowered its gorgeous head, and she laid her hand on its nose. Neither one of them noticed me, and I felt like I was looking at something private, something I ought not to be seeing. The unicorn, in case you've never seen one (which is actually pretty likely) wasn't anything like a white horse. I mean, it was horse shaped, in that Jon Hamm is monkey shaped, but you'd never mistake one for the other. It wasn't even white. It was silver, or mother of pearl. Its nose and feet were darker silver, and it was surrounded by rainbows shimmering off its body like they do over water sometimes. It did have a horn, though, and that was made of light. It was too bright to look at.

After a minute of the girl and the unicorn looking at each other, and me looking at them, three men in black clothes came out from the shadows between the cars. One had a rope. One had some sort of industrial looking oven mitts; elbow length ones, like glassblowers use. When I saw what else he had, I thought I was going to throw up. He had a hacksaw. The unicorn saw them, too, and it began to shiver. But it looked like the stories were true the ones about unicorns and purity. I guessed right away the girl was a virgin, I remembered the story from those tapestries—you can still seem them, I think they're hanging in a museum in New York. That's how you're supposed to be able to catch a unicorn—get a virgin to snare it. As long as the girl was touching it, it couldn't move to save itself other than shift from side to side and stamp its feet. Two of them went to its head, and the guy with the gauntlets pulled the horn down far enough for the guy with the rope to get a loop around it. The other went to its side and put his hands on it, I guess to make it stop moving around. Black smoke blotted out the rainbows, and it began to make a noise that if I'm super lucky I'll never hear again. The guy slapped its smoking side and laughed. That guy had his back to me.

So I made a decision that honestly, I knew was pretty stupid, but wouldn't you have done the same? Wouldn't anyone?

I got my garlic spray out of my pocket and slowly stood up. The girl looked almost hypnotized, and the two guys at the unicorn's head were busy getting the rope tied to it, so they were all busy. I squeezed between the two cars I'd been hiding behind, and then I walked up to the guy nearest me and tapped him on the shoulder. When he turned, I blasted him in the face with the garlic spray. Now, he wasn't a vamp, but I get the spray from a guy online who weaponizes it with a blend of Carolina Reaper and Ghost peppers, and it doesn't matter who or what you are, you're going down. He did, clutching his face and howling.

The girl looked under the unicorn's trembling neck and saw me and the man rolling in circles and holding his head, and she screamed. So did I. She must have yanked her hand back just enough to break whatever magic spell was going on, because the unicorn lifted its head and gave a huge, ringing bellow, and flicked the rope off of its horn, rearing up on its back feet. As it did, it clipped the guy with the rope in the forehead with one of its shining hooves. That guy went down, too, and harder. There was a lot of blood.

I don't know what happened next, because the flash of light from the explosion was too bright. It was like a transformer blew up. When I could see again, the unicorn was gone. I got up off the ground and ran to the girl. I thought maybe the men were holding her captive, or something.

"Let's get out of here." I held out my hand.

She pushed her glorious long blonde hair out of her face and blinked her huge blue eyes at me. "You stupid fucking bitch! What the hell are you doing? Do you know how much money you just cost me?"

So she wasn't a captive. Now, I wasn't a fan of the xenos wandering the streets in those days, but what I really hated were poachers. Too many actual people got killed when the xenos fought back. Of course, if you asked them, the xenos weren't the guests, or the strangers (that's what xeno means in Latin) we mortal humans were, despite what we decided to call the various tribes of fairy tale creatures—from elves to werewolves to unicorns—who revealed themselves all at once. They'd been here all along. Mortals trying to turn a profit on them was a slightly more recent development.

I held my hands up, palms facing out. "I already called the cops," I said.

The third guy had stuffed his crying, red-faced friend into the back of their car, and was trying to drag the one with the head wound in. "Margaret," he hissed, "let's get out of here. We'll get it another night."

She turned away, but stopped long enough to give me the finger. "See you soon, bitch." She hopped in the car, a piece of crap Honda with Maryland plates, and they were gone. Nothing left but a black, oily puddle in the road.

I took a couple of deep breaths. No sirens, I obviously hadn't called anyone, but with all that noise someone would be on their way, and soon. I hurried back towards my car.

If you got dragged to museums all your young life like I did, you've probably seen a statue called The Dying Gaul. If not, you've probably seen a picture of it. It's basically a big naked dude with a mortal injury. For a second, I thought someone had dropped that statue on Kenyon Street, and propped it against my car. It took another second to realize that first—this was an alive person, not a statue, and two— no beard and no broken sword. He sure was naked, though. In the light from the streetlamp his skin looked almost like silvery marble. That must have been why I thought of the statue.

I came up a little closer. He was clutching his side and panting, his hair was plastered to his scalp and stuck to his neck. I asked maybe the stupidest question possible, but what are your options?

"Dude, are you okay?"

His eyes flew open. "Don't touch me."

"Wasn't going to. Do you, um, need an ambulance or something?" I carefully reached around him and recovered my purse. "Did you see what just happened?"

He got to his feet. His legs were shaking and he was holding his side, and he was still super naked. "What? No. I just got here."

"Right." I got a towel out of the back of the Mini and shook bits of leaves and grit out. I handed it to him and when he took it, I saw a huge purple-black bruise on his ribs. "Damn, did you get hit by a car or something?"

"Something," he agreed vaguely. He looked pretty woozy and I was afraid he might pass out.

"I really think I should call you an ambulance."

"No," he said. "You. Can you help me?" And he looked at me in a way that made me think I'd never been seen before. The way your oldest friend looks at you, who knows all your secrets and loves you anyway. Your mother. Someone you trust. And the next thing I knew he was in in the passenger seat with his head back and his eyes closed, and I was driving back up 16th and heading for my apartment in Columbia Heights.

There was plenty to complain about with my apartment—the water pressure was more like a dainty trickle, and there were rats and Kagkai in the alley, but one thing I couldn't find fault with was the parking spot that led directly to the staircase to my second floor entryway. With my hours and what's out there I couldn't be trolling for parking all night. Anyway, I had a back door for a front door, and so no one saw wrapped-in-a-towel guy and me go inside.

"You want a beer?" I asked, which seemed to be the polite thing to do. The sensible thing would have been to call the police or an ambulance, but all I can say is I didn't want to upset him. I know, it sounds nuts. Anyway, he agreed a beer would be good. When he reached out to take the bottle, I saw the blood on his hand. While he was drinking, I took a pic of him.

"Why did you do that?" he asked.

"I take a picture of everyone who comes over," I lied. He frowned like he didn't believe me, but was too tired to argue.

"Can I use your shower? I have dirt from the ground on me. And. . ." he lifted his bloody hand and looked at it. "I must have cut myself. When I fell."

"In the car accident. Sure." I didn't think it was his blood, but I was pretty tired, too. "There's clean towels hanging on the back of the door."

I heard the door click shut and the shower begin to run. I got myself another beer and texted my best friend Marly. I knew she'd probably be up; for a middle school English teacher, grading papers was like a second full time job. I sent the picture and typed:

> **Strange hot dude in shower. If I get murdered it was him**

She texted back three eggplants and a question mark. For a lover of language she adapted to texting pretty fast.

> **Come by Hare 2morrow & find out**

> **Proud of U for getting back on the horse!**

Marly knew it had been a while—a long while—since anything like this had happened to me. She'd tried to set me up with everyone from her assistant principle (nose hair issue) to the woman who delivers her mail (Cait is cute but I'm not into girls. I'm really not into anything, I guess).

The water stopped, and he came out wearing the same towel as went he went in with. He was pulling his clean hands through his hair, which was longer than I thought, shiny and dark.

"I like that," I said, pointing at the silver streak that fell in a damp curl over his right eye. "Very Rogue." He looked at me blankly. "From the X-Men?" Nothing. "Okay, so very Bonnie Raitt, then."

He smiled for the first time, and that was a whole different thing. It was an actual jolt. "Angel From Montgomery," he said. "I. . .I spend a lot of time in the mountains. The Schind-han-do-wi. I, um, camped near people who liked to sing that song."

"Schin. . .Shenandoah?"

"I'm pretty sure that's not how you pronounce it," he informed me. Then he yawned so hard I thought he was going to dislocate his jaw.

"Look," I said, "my eyes are slamming shut. Let me get you a blanket and find you something to wear. I have to get to sleep. Are you going to be okay?"

He gave me that look again. "I'll be fine. I'm feeling better."

I dug out an old pair of stretched out sweatpants and an XL University of Miami t shirt, and handed them over. As I did, our hands brushed. I didn't do it on purpose, I actually forgot what he said about not touching him. But he yelped and jumped back, dropping the clothes.

"Jeez, what was that?" I bent to pick them up. He was staring at his hand.

"It was nothing," he said, looking at it as if he were surprised it was still attached to his wrist. "Nothing at all. I'm sorry."

By the time I pulled out clean sheets and a blanket for the couch, he was already stretched out and asleep with an arm flung over his face. Normally I don't notice them, but I have to say he had very nice feet. Wherever he came from, he was getting pedicures on the regular. Before I threw the blanket over him, I took another picture. Then I shut the light and went back to my bedroom. Despite the nice feet and the even nicer smile, I locked my door. I scrolled to the second picture. The bruise on his side was definitely smaller—in fact, it was almost gone.

There was already weak sunlight coming in from under the blinds when I set my phone down and turn out the light. That was when I realized I never asked his name.

2

I **was dreaming about running through** a forest. I couldn't tell what was chasing me, but I knew they'd never catch me. I could hear bells ringing in the distance. Then the bells sounded again, much closer. It was my phone, the alarm on my phone, and I was pitched out of the woods and into my room. I had a dozen texts from Marly.

> **RU murdered?**
>
> **If not murdered**
> **how was?**
>
> **RU in sex coma?**
>
> **txt me right now!**

And more eggplants and question marks. She was really invested in my lack of a sex life. I shot her a quick note saying I was alive and to come see me, but I had to head in for my shift. My guest was still out cold on the couch with the blanket over his head. I could see he was breathing, so I left a note saying I was at work and he could eat whatever was in the fridge. I know it was a stupid move, leaving a stranger alone in my house, but he'd already not stabbed me or stolen my TV. Anyway, I wanted to find out what happened to him; I felt sort of responsible. And the way he looked at me...

For a nice change of pace I got a spot only a block from the bar where I worked. It was officially called The Tortoise and The Hare; The Tortoise was the restaurant downstairs, and The Hare was my nightly domain. It was the second floor of the small rowhouse, just a narrow bar with a dozen barstools, and little round tables for a dozen more. We had a nice window over the street and another over the alley, and a decent sound system. It had been my home for the three years I'd lived in DC.

Once I said hello to Zonia the afternoon hostess, I headed up the steps to The Hare. I was happy to see my friend Claudio working as my barback. The other barback, Davy, wore too much cologne and showed off his buttcrack whenever he bent to pick something up, which was constantly. Claudio was cutting limes when I walked in, fragrant and sharp, and the small bar smelled as good as it ever did. It wouldn't have that stale beer perfume until after we closed at 2am.

"Dude," I said, "You are never going to guess what happened to me last night."

He swung his long braid back over his shoulder, set

down the knife and said, "Love, twue love?"

"Ha, no. I rescued a unicorn."

He squinted at me. "Is that code for something?"

"No, a real unicorn. On the street, up the block. Some poachers were going to saw its fucking horn off, and I chased them away."

"Dude," he said gravely. "That is intense. For real? What did it look like? They're super rare, right?"

"It was the most beautiful thing I've ever seen. For real. I can't understand how anyone would want to hurt something as. . .I don't know. As perfect as that."

"Dollars. I hear the horns are worth, like, the gross national product of a medium sized country. So the poachers must be mega pissed at you, huh?"

"I guess. I maced one of them, so he probably isn't inviting me to the prom. The girl—they had an actual virgin, can you believe it? She was beyond mad at me." I paused. "And I think the unicorn might have killed one of the dudes. It kicked him in the head."

"What happened to it?" Claudio's eyes were wide. "Did it say thank you?"

I shook my head. The whole thing seemed fuzzy, like remembering a dream. "It literally went up in a puff of smoke. I hope it's okay."

"Huh. Crazy night."

"Oh, that's just the beginning. I went back to my car after the poachers took off, and there was a naked guy lying in the road. I think he got hit by a car." I frowned. "Maybe the poachers hit him. He was pretty shook up."

"So," Claudio said, "the unicorn disappeared, and this dude showed up like two minutes later?"

"That's exactly what happened."

"He just happened to appear--—"

"Yeah, it was lucky for him I was there. He was pretty beat up." I pulled out my phone and showed Claudio the picture—the first one, not the the sleeping one. I didn't want him to think I was a creeper. "He's at my house."

"Holy shit," he said admiringly.

"I know, right?"

"And you left him at your house? Alone? Can I go make sure he's okay?" I guess Claudio has a type, although tall, dark and cute is pretty much the O+ of types.

I laughed. "Make sure you get his name, I forgot to ask."

He shook his head. "Just call him Sweetie. That's what I do."

The afternoon crowd wandered in, people did what normal people do, and eventually it was dusk. Nothing weird took place. I was beginning to think the whole experience really had been a dream—stranger things have happened, right? Although, if Part One was a dream, Part Two—Couch Guy—was probably also a dream. I hoped not—I was kind of looking forward to seeing the cute guy on my couch when I got home. I was also looking forward to his answering a few questions. There had to be a good explanation for what happened to him. I was starting to put together a theory. It had to do with a vengeful girlfriend, a fight, and a sharp blow to the head. Maybe she hid his clothes before she threw him out, and he stumbled into traffic. I didn't have an explanation for the disappearing black and blue mark, though. Or the blood on his hand. Or the fear I saw on his face when I found him. Fear, and guilt.

I was pouring a bourbon and ginger when things took a turn. At the same time I noticed an ache behind my eyes, I smelled garbage. I glanced at the can behind the bar. Only half full. I looked around for the source of the stink and that's when I saw the vamp standing in the doorway. She was pretty, like they mostly all are objectively attractive, but of course she smelled like trash. I mean, she was dead. There were a lot of disappointed Twilight fans when the xenos revealed themselves.

"Oh, no fucking way. Get out or I'm calling the cops."

The dead girl giggled and held up her hands in a way that was supposed to be calming. "Just here to talk, honey." She smirked at me with her pallid, perfect face. "Not like the other time." Other kinds of xenos use vamps as messengers, so it may have been true that she only wanted to talk. They move fast, they have no fear, and they'll do anything to get paid—in blood, of course. The downside is they're all completely insane. I pulled out my garlic spray. "We don't allow your kind in here, freak. Get out." The thing about them not being able to enter a dwelling until you invite them? Wishful thinking, unfortunately.

The regulars began edging for the exits.

I tried to control my breathing, hyperventilate too long and you'll pass out. I ran through the mantra Dr. Bel taught me: *I'm alive, I'm in my body. I have control. I'm alive, I'm in my body. . .*

Claudio had one hand in his hair and was mumbling the Lord's Prayer. He had charms, motifs, symbols, and blessed relics from every religion I've ever heard of tied into his long, braided ponytail. He gets a box of new ones from his Nonna in Brooklyn a couple of times a year. That, to me, makes sense. Some people vouched for just carrying a cross, but that only works if you run into a vamp who had been baptized before getting turned. What if you get attacked by an atheist? Wave a copy of On The Origin of Species at it? If you're going with icons, all in or nothing. Since I fall on the side of 'nothing' I carried garlic spray.

One thing vamps can do other than stink up the joint is move fast, like so fast you can't see them. She did that now, and went from the top of the stairs to the bar in less than a second. "We want the horse," she said. "Give it over. Where is the horse?"

"What are you talking about, Crazy? Do you see a horse in here?"

She did the speed move again, and had my phone in her hand. "Here," she said. She held it up. It was the picture of my couch guy. "We want the horse," she repeated, and tapped the screen. It scrolled to the picture of him sleeping. "Pretty, pretty horse," she said. She squinted at the picture. "And you called me a freak. Heh." The she furrowed her brow and stared at me with those blank, glittery eyes. She was thinking hard, trying to remember what to say with whatever was left inside her head. "They said to tell you that you can't protect it. They said you should stay out of it. That you should know better after last time. They'll have it no matter what you do. And if you don't give it to them, I get to eat you!" Her brow smoothed and she twirled around the room to the music playing over the speakers. Frank Ocean. "No no! Don't give it to them after all! You're so delicious!" The way she was moving stirred the air and the smell was making my eyes water. She stopped mid-twirl. "But the pretty horse, he's delicious too. I'm gonna go find him. Pretty horse. See you soon!"

She was gone.

"I'm gonna be sick." Claudio got up from where he'd been wedged between the ice cooler and the beer kegs. "Sorry, babe. I hate those things." He touched my shoulder. "I know you do, too. You okay? Need a Xanax?" I said I was fine. "You sure?"

He nodded at my hands. I was gripping the spray bottle so tightly I bent the plastic lid. "Just give me a minute."

Claudio looked around the room at the remaining patrons, who were now mostly staring at me. "Free Fireball and PBRs for anyone who opens a window." He got my phone off the bar, didn't comment on the photo, and wiped it off with a clean bar rag before handing it back to me. "Why did she say that? About your friend?"

If they found me, they knew where I lived.

"Shit, oh my god. I gotta go. Can you watch the bar?"

"Sure, of course." He reached into his long hair. "Take this. Please." He unknotted a silver crucifix. "I know it's not what you're into, but I'll feel better."

I thanked him and shoved it in my pocket and ran for

my car, hoping I wasn't too late. Too late for what, I didn't quite know.

3

By the time I got home, I was in an absolute lather. Traffic on 14th Street was even more jacked up than usual, and I hit every red light before I made it to my alley. I came to halt on my way up the stairs. The back door was open. And I smelled garbage.

"I am alive; I am in my body. . ."

I wanted to run away, but I kept picturing the vamp girl tapping my guy's picture with her dirty fingernail. I pulled the little cross and my spray out of my pocket and crept inside. The smell was stronger in here, but it was quiet. The couch was unoccupied, and the blanket was neatly folded. Crazy vamp girl wouldn't have been so tidy, and there'd be blood sprayed on the walls. Vamps are enthusiastic feeders.

"Above and Below, what's that smell?"

I spun on my heel and almost blasted couch guy in the

face with the garlic spray.

"Oh my god, I thought you were dead." I threw my arms around him and I'm embarrassed to admit, I started crying. He didn't flinch or jump back when I grabbed him, he just stood there with his arms at his sides. He was holding a plastic grocery bag with a smiley face on it in one hand and a coffee in the other. I let him go and he put his purchases on the table.

"Why would you think that? Why are you upset? And really, what is making that smell?"

"No, me first. Let's start with your name."

"Can I eat and talk?" I nodded, wiping my face, and he sat. "My name is March." He looked around the room and made a face. "I changed my mind, can we open some windows?" He got back up and we went through the house opening windows and turning on fans. When the funk had cleared out, he sat back down at my tiny kitchen table and pulled the sweat pants and t-shirt out of the grocery bag, along with his dinner in a white paper sack. "Thank you for the clothing."

He was now wearing worn but clean jeans and an oatmeal colored henley, along with faded black chucks with no laces. "Where did you get those clothes?" I knew he didn't have any money unless his wallet was very well hidden, and my TV and laptop were still where I left them.

He smiled. "Ercilia gave them to me. She's very nice."

"Ercilia from the bodega? She wouldn't even give me a dirty look for free. Did you steal them?"

He pulled two arepas and a slice of tres leches cake out

of the paper bag. "She gave me this, too. Told me to come back any time. Want some?"

I shook my head and watched him eat. He finished the cake and unselfconsciously licked the sweetness off his fingers. That was a sight to behold.

"March, huh?"

"March," he repeated. "What about you?"

He looked at me with those green-brown eyes and I swear I would have told him my whole life story, anything he wanted to know, and handed him my bra for an encore, but instead I said, "Ruby. And the smell was a vamp. Vampire. Ever seen one?"

He set his coffee down. "Yes. Unpleasant. Why are there vampires coming to your house, Ruby?"

It was kind of difficult to concentrate on the story, the way he said my name. He didn't have an accent, but there was something he did to the words that made them. . .blurry? Soft? I gave my head a shake and said, "I think it might have something to do with you. One came to the bar and said she was looking for a horse. She saw the picture I took of you, and said you were a horse. Why did she say that?"

He laughed. "I'm obviously not a horse."

Despite his panty melting voice and scorching hot looks, I was getting annoyed. It was getting hard to breathe. "You haven't told me what happened to you. Or where the bruise on your side went. Or how you got all that stuff from Ercilia. And yeah, I can see you're not a horse, but that vamp thought—"

"Don't you know?" He looked at me with genuine

curiosity. "Surely you do."

"Know what?" I was getting a headache from this.

He leaned forward. "You know, I never thanked you for saving me last night."

"I didn't save you, I just gave you a towel and let you use my shower." Definitely a headache, and a little nauseated. "You crashed on my couch and next you'll tell me about the fight with your girlfriend..."

"It was foolish of you to take on those men. They could have hurt you. But you saved my life, and I am in your debt." I put my hands over my ears like a three-year-old. "Look at me. You know it's true." I shook my head. "Why don't you want it to be true?" he asked.

I looked up and took a big breath so I wouldn't pass out. "Because if you're. . .if you aren't just a guy who had a fight with his girlfriend, then this time it's my fault because this time I invited you in."

"What's your fault?? Will you tell me?" he asked in that warm, sweet voice. Honey, it was like honey in my head. It made the sick feeling go away.

I took a deep breath. "I will. Just, not right now, okay?"

He agreed. "Just as long as it's not me who is causing you distress."

"No. No, it's definitely not you." I cleared my throat. *I am alive.* "So. You're a. . ."

"A unicorn."

"Wow."

"You know this, you saw me."

"You really said it."

"Until early this morning."

"There's a unicorn in my kitchen. That's new."

"There isn't, though. Not anymore. Now I'm. . ." He looked down at his body. "I'm this mortal person."

"Can you change back and forth? Like a werewolf or something?"

He looked offended. "They are a different class of creature altogether. But yes, I can—I could. I've been a man many times through the years. I've always found it illuminating."

"You weren't camping in the forest, were you? When you heard music?" I imagined a unicorn grooving to someone's boom box, hidden in a grove of trees.

He shook his head. "That was my home. I lived in those mountains before any humans came there. I used to be able to run from the ocean to the big river without ever seeing another creature who walked on two legs. Those are days that won't come again."

That made him pre-pre-Colombian. "How old are you?"

He shrugged. "I don't know. Is it important?" I said I guessed it wasn't. "That was one of the reasons I learned how to put on a body like this. I could see the world changing, and I wanted to walk in it. I wanted to hear music. And food—I like your food. And other things." He sighed. "I suppose I'd better get used to this."

"Why? Can't you just change back? Why are you still even here?"

"Because of what happened last night. I took a life. I killed that man." He looked at his hands again, at where the blood had been.

"It was an accident," I said. "Wasn't it? You were defending yourself. And what does that have to do with your, um, shape?"

"Whether or not it was an accident, it was my fault. Only one who is pure can be what I was. I'm a lesser thing, now." I thought about the glorious creature I'd seen last night, and the ordinary man sitting at the table. He must have still been in shock a little bit and it hadn't sunk in, because if it was me, I would have been crying, under the bed, forever. He just looked sad.

"So you're stuck like this?"

He nodded. "I think I am."

"I'm sorry. But I guess that means whoever was looking for you won't be interested anymore."

"Well, they may not know that. They may think I am choosing to hide in this body. That's probably why the vampire came to your bar." He sighed. "Did the thing say who hired her?"

"No. Sorry."

He shrugged. "I wouldn't have known them anyway. I don't know anyone, really. My folk stay well out of sight. It can be many years between meetings." He cocked his head. "That's why I was there last night. I heard one of my own was looking for me. Somehow they knew it was the only thing that would have brought me here, to see another. . ." He ran a hand through his hair. "It's a good thing I like the food, huh?" He gave a strange, biting laugh and ran his hand over his face. "Would you excuse me?"

He closed the bathroom door, and I got myself a beer

and thought about what he'd said. It was a small place, and I tried not to listen—ran water in the sink, even—but I think he was crying.

I guess it finally sunk in.

4

e are rare, but we are there.

When was the first time you heard that phrase? Probably about eight years ago, right? And then it just stopped. You want to know why? It was because of me.

When they started revealing themselves I was a freshman at the University of Miami. I had a sweet apartment at the un-chic edge of Coral Gables. I had a boyfriend and a job at a boutique and no prescription for Xanax. I didn't have a scar or a standing appointment with a therapist. I read about the xenos online; first just the tabloidy sites, then the New York Times and the Miami Herald and CNN and everywhere else. They couldn't deny it: fairy tale creatures were real. There were pics of selkies and werewolves and elves. Michael Moore made a documentary—I didn't see it, though. I never saw a xeno, as they were called, so I thought it was pretty cool and kind of filed it away. I looked for mermaids when I went to the beach, like everyone else, but never saw one. They were rare, like they said. As the months went by and the movement grew bigger, they started talking about voting rights and stuff like that. I remember reading on D-Listed that a troll got hired as a bodyguard for Mariah Carey, and everyone thought that was hilarious. It was mostly the were-folk and fairies that were the face of the movement—the ones that already lived at least part time as regular people and would have the best chance at assimilating. I remember seeing a beautiful woman with a sort of green tint on the news, I think she was a dryad. The talk show hosts loved her. It seemed like they were getting some momentum.

I'm the reason they stopped.

I was taking out the garbage when it happened. I didn't pay any attention to the smell, because I was standing next to the dumpster, and of course it smelled like garbage. But three of them, three vamps, had me on my back between one breath and the next. If it had been a movie, the vampire slaying heroine would have heard a scream from an alley, but by the time she arrived, it was too late—another victim, another dead girl, her throat ripped open and drained of blood. The star of the movie would shake her head and swear that she'd get the bastards who did this, and that would be the end. Oh, first they'd cut my head off and burn my body, *that* would be the end.

It didn't work out like that.

Now, vamps had been attacking people since forever, but this was for the public. This was for show. I didn't find out until much later, but if they had been even a little bit organized I would have been left with my throat torn out in the middle of Biscayne Boulevard, but like I said, they're all crazy. So instead of making some sort of statement about vamps and humans, instead they began fighting over me, and one of them fell against a garbage can. My landlady Mrs. Flores heard something, bless her nosy-no-air-conditioning heart. She grabbed a broom and went to chase away the raccoons she thought were in the trash. When she opened her door, the porch light came on and they scattered. She found me and called 911. They saved my life—barely.

This was the early days of xenomedicine, so they did some things they wouldn't necessarily do anymore. I mean, they know now you won't turn if you just get bitten, although you may 'exhibit some traits consistent with xenobiology'. It's almost always temporary.

I was in the hospital for three months, and for the first month they kept me in isolation in a dark room, because I screamed my head off every time someone put on a light. I was also under constant observation and in restraints because they didn't know if I was going to turn. I don't blame them; I didn't know either. And because vamps are filthy, I got every kind of antibiotic they could lay their hands on. I also got a rabies series, antivirals, typhoid, yellow fever, malaria (I'm not sure why they thought I was going to get malaria, it wasn't a mosquito bite) and tetanus. My neck was such a mess I needed four surgeries and a couple of laser treatments. Even so, it's still hot and crawly and looks pretty gross, so I wear my hair forward.

I told my friends and my parents and the therapist I

didn't remember it, it was just a blur, I was out of it most of the time. But the fact is I remember everything from what their breath smelled like (don't let anyone tell you vamps don't breathe) to what their teeth felt like, to what the immuno-globulin series felt like, to wondering what I would be when I woke up. Because I was too scared to go to sleep, I had a lot of time to think.

They finally sent me home, satisfied I wasn't going to turn into a monster, but the story had legs, as they say, and I was on the news a couple of times. That's when I found out I was supposed to be a manifesto. I never talked to the reporters. My landlady did, though. After that, a bunch of morons decided they were going to be vampire slayers, and went around looking for something to kill. There have always been vampire hunters, just like there have always been vampires, but these guys had cameras and live feeds. I kept track—one stabbed his brother who was pranking him by pretending to be a vamp, two injured homeless guys, one staked his girlfriend by accident and then tried to kill himself, and one unlucky bastard actually found a vamp, which immediately ate him. I guess watching someone get their throat torn out for real is different than seeing it in a movie.

There wasn't any more xeno rights movement after that. I think even that poor troll got fired.

The worst part for me was the smell. I couldn't get it off me. I took a lot of baths, and I did a lot of thinking. I thought about why I was alive, and the vampire hunter's girlfriend wasn't. I thought about what I smelled like. I sat in the bathtub and thought, and wondered. Eventually my parents had to go back north, they both worked and family leave ran out. My boyfriend, all my friends, they all got tired of me thinking, and asking them if I smelled bad. I thought my way right out of school.

Again, Mrs. Flores stepped in. She gave me a business card and told me she'd evict me if I didn't see the doctor who took care of her grandson who got an STD and a broken heart from a lamia. The doctor was a specialist in a new field: xeno psychotrauma. Dr. Bel was the next one to rescue me. I remember the first few times I saw her, I just sat in her office and cried and begged her to tell me if I stank. She taught me how to get out of the circle where those thoughts lived, and what to tell myself when I smelled something bad. She gave me that mantra. She also gave me the web address of the guy with the garlic spray. When she relocated her practice to Washington DC, I followed. I still see her sometimes. After my night with the unicorn I felt like maybe I'd need to see her soon.

***

March came out of the bathroom and apologized for his outburst. I told him it wasn't much of an outburst and he had every right to be upset. Then I sat him on the couch and told him what had happened to me. "So," I finished, "I know a little something about feeling responsible for something you had no control over."

"I'm so sorry, Ruby," March said. "Thank you for telling me." Then he pushed my hair back and looked at my torn-up neck. It was the first time he'd touched me on purpose. He laid his hand on the scar, and it went from its usual hot, itchy, crawling, to cool. It felt like nothing ever happened. He dropped his hand and I missed it right away. My neck began to burn and tingle again. "Of course, we aren't—"

"I know you aren't all like that. It's unfair to think so."

He shook his head. "That isn't what I was going to say. I was going to say we aren't meant to be known. When I heard about what my kind were trying to do, I thought it was a terrible idea, and I wasn't the only one. It's like those misguided slayers you talked about—they think they know us, and people get killed. My people and yours. We are a danger to each other."

"I'm glad you're here," I blurted. It didn't seem like the right thing to say after being told you're dangerous, but it was true. "I'm not sorry I'm alive, and I'm also not sorry it was that guy with the saw last night and not you. But we can't stay here hiding out. I have to go back to work, and I want you to come with me."

"You think the vampire will come back?"

"I think someone will."

Before we left I dug my kit out from under the bed. There's no foolproof way to keep vamps out if they want something, but you can sure as fuck slow them down. I propped my big mirror just inside the front door, so you could see yourself from the stoop. They don't like mirrors. You can't see their reflections, but they can and apparently they are either repulsed or seduced by their own image. Either way it's like flypaper. There's some debate, but I've heard running water also can work. I had a pair of cat drinking fountains I set end to end just inside the door—couldn't hurt, might help. And garlic of course, I hung my garlands around the door and the windows. Fresh is best but dried is also good. A stake through the heart would have ended that girl's post-mortem career, but getting a stick of wood through the sternum of something that's fighting back is just about impossible without a crossbow. They offer self-defense classes, and I tried. Turn out I'm not an MMA fighter; so best to stop them before they get close, or even better, before they get inside.

I turned all the lights on, and I plugged in the DarkAway SAD No More lamps I picked up from the same web site as the garlic spray. I'm afraid I went slightly overboard—I have five of them. One for every room in the house including the bathroom, and a motion sensor over the back door. My electric bill was going to be bonkers, but it was worth it. The last thing I did was lock the windows and pull all the shades. From the outside I could see the brilliant white light leaking under the drapes. I thought it would do.

March was shooting me looks as we walked down the steps to my car, like maybe I was just as big a threat as the vamps. Crazy humans could be unpredictable, right?

"Hey," I said, "at least I don't cover the windows with tinfoil."

He looked dubious. "Does that work?"

"Ask my ex. According to him it was to keep out aliens."

His eyes got wide. "There are aliens?"

"Only when he was off his meds." You aren't supposed to date people you're in group therapy with, as it turns out, for a good reason. Those bitches are crazy.

good reason. Those bitches are crazy.

5

e finally got back to The Hare close to midnight, and the place was pretty full. Claudio spotted me and a wave of relief crossed his face. He preferred to barback; he didn't have a good memory for orders and drink recipes, he hated making change, and anyway it was too busy for one person to handle. I slid behind the bar, and to my surprise, three people got up from their stools to offer March a place to sit. He wasn't even a pregnant lady or a celebrity.

"I am so sorry, Clo, please don't kill me," I said, pressing the little silver cross back into his hand. But Claudio wasn't looking at me.

"You must be car accident couch guy," he said.

March smiled and introduced himself, and Claudio blushed. He actually blushed.

"What the hell, dude." I whacked his shoulder and he jumped.

"Nice to meet you," he stammered. "Want a beer? Or something else? Can I get you a menu? Or some water?"

Never mind that there were like twenty people waving money at him. I gave a sigh and went to work. I didn't get a chance to slow down and talk to either one of them, and when Marly came in, I could only wave and point to where March was drinking bourbon. I did notice a rough semi-circle of customers gathered behind him, just watching him. In fact, it looked like everyone in the place was sneaking looks at him, if not openly gazing. And people were sending him drinks; there was a line of shots of bourbon in front of him. Marly plopped herself down, helped herself to a shot (no one else was brave enough to sit next to him) and began texting.

My phone went off.

????!!!!!

I replied.

¯_(ツ)_/¯

I kept one eye on the two of them. There was a lot of laughing and nodding and some shoulder slapping, followed by lowered heads and serious faces. The bar folks also watched the pair, and I swear some of them didn't even stop to blink. I wondered what they thought they saw, and why Marly seemed blithely indifferent to whatever it was he did to everyone else. Maybe it was their shared love of bourbon?

Finally, it was last call, and like we always did we put on

The Wreck of The Edmund Fitzgerald. By the time the last brave sailor's lungs filled with the icy water of Lake Superior, the place was empty except for Claudio, Marly, March and me. I locked the door and gratefully sat down. I was whipped; the last two days had seemed endless.

"So," Marly said. "Your boyfriend here is a unicorn. Well played."

"He is not my—you told her?" Marly could be pretty persuasive; classrooms full of twelve year olds had turned her into Mother Superior Drill Sargent. Between that and the bourbon, it was no wonder he'd spilled.

March shrugged. "She asked what my story was." He turned back to her. "I did tell you I'm not one anymore, right?"

Claudio nodded sagely. "He's under a curse." His Nonna was going to love this.

"It's not really a curse." March finished the last of his drink. "This is so good. Is there any more?" I guess he didn't understand the main purpose of a bar.

Claudio looked at me. "I'm not his mother," I said. He poured.

"Thank you." He smiled at Claudio again, and poor Clo visibly melted. I'd have to talk to him. "I was. . .I guess you could say I was demoted. When Ruby rescued me—" and when he looked at me, *I* blushed. Jesus Christ on a literal cracker, it was like being under a heat lamp, the way he looked at a person. "When she rescued me I. . .something happened, and this is my punishment. My judgement. I am a debased, lesser creature. You know, like you."

We all let that one sit there for a minute.

"'Something' happened?" Marly frowned. "It must have been something pretty intense. What did you do, kill a guy?"

March looked stricken. It was all I could do not to throw myself on top of him, like Marly was a grenade.

"Leave it," I said. "He doesn't want to talk about it. We're just trying to figure out what to do next."

"You should take him to see your doctor," said Claudio. "She always seems to help you."

That was a smart idea. "You're right," I said. "March, what do you think? Would you like to talk to my doctor?"

"What's wrong with me isn't a malady of the flesh," he said mournfully. He seemed equally saddened about his human condition and his nearly empty drink, and he held the glass back out. Claudio would probably have walked to Kentucky to get him a refill at this point; he didn't consult me this time as he poured.

"Well, I understand that," I told March. "We have doctors now that work on, um, maladies of the mind."

He rolled his eyes. "I know what a therapist is."

"Well, how am I supposed to know everything you're up to date on?"

"He didn't know who the Kardashians were," Marly added. "I was jealous." She turned back to him. "So can I ask you a question?" March nodded warily. "What's the deal with virgins?"

"Oh my god, Marly." I was going to kill her.

"I don't know," he said. "I mean, yes, they are the only mortal people who can touch us. When I'm in my real body, not when I'm like this. And they have power over us, I just don't know why that should be. That's why I couldn't get away when she had her hand on me. The girl—"

"Margaret," I said. "Her name was. Mean as a fucking snake." Sooner or later she'd be back around. Would she still have a hold on him?

"Right. Her body was pure, but her soul was wicked." He shook his head. "You'd think it would be the other way around, but I don't make the rules." Marly started asking him something about Pliny, and I excused myself.

While they were talking, I called my doctor's answering service, and left a voice mail. "Hi, Doctor Bel," I said. "I know I haven't been by to see you lately but something has come up. I have a friend who really could use your help. He's been hurt, and I think he's having a hard time dealing with the fallout. I'd super appreciate it if you could see him—"

My phone chimed. "Ruby, tell me about your friend."

Dr. Bel never lets me down. I'd gotten calls from her around the clock, whenever I needed her. I could sleep better knowing she was there. But this fast, this was a surprise.

"Really sorry to bother you. I know it's late."

"It's no bother, honey. Now, what happened to your friend? You say he was attacked by a xeno?"

"No. He *is* the xeno."

There was a long pause. "And you say he's your friend? Are you all right yourself?"

"I'm...I'm better than he is. Can I bring him to see you?"

Another pause. I could hear her flipping pages. "You'd better both come in tomorrow. Noon?"

I thanked her and rang off. "We're going to see her

tomorrow, so let's get this place closed up and get home." Claudio was wiping down the bar and Marly had grabbed a broom, bless her. I put clean glasses away and covered the leftover fruit to stick in the fridge.

March, who had been raptly watching the ice in the cooler melt, set his glass carefully on the bar and looked at me. "Then I'll stay with you?"

I'm not going to lie. I know he was a little drunk and pretty traumatized, and Dr. Bel has told me that's a vulnerable place to be, but I just wanted to kiss him so damned bad.

"Yes," I said. "You'll stay with me."

An hour later and we were on the steps outside my apartment. I hesitated unlocking the door even though all the lights were still on and nothing seemed wrong. With the events of the last few days playing like a movie in my mind, I didn't want to go inside and find anything unwelcome waiting for me.

I took a big sniff just in case. "Do you smell anything?"

"Yes," March said. "I can smell you."

I jerked my head up, startled. Pain and shame bloomed in my chest, I hadn't felt them for a long time. Tears stung my eyes. But he continued. "Rosemary. In your soap, I think? I can smell it on you. I could smell you all night." He leaned closer to me, I could feel his warm breath on my cheek. "You smell so good." The pain went away but it was replaced by something else, something just as strong. Stronger. Something I also hadn't felt for a while. "Ruby," he said, in a soft voice that made me shiver. "Ruby?"

"Yes?" I whispered.

"Are you going to open the door?"

I snapped out of it and fumbled my keys out of my bag and let us in. Everything was in place, all the lights, the water fountains and the ropes of garlic. March helped me move the mirror out of the way, and it was hard not to stare at our reflections—at his reflection, right over my shoulder. He'd for sure picked a perfect body to be stuck in. Then he caught me looking, and I blushed for the second time that day. I don't think I've blushed that much in the last ten years, but the way he looked at me, with those forest colored eyes. . .*I am in my body*. . . I wasn't even sure if what I was feeling was panic, or the hot rush of being alive.

"I'm gonna take a quick shower," I told him, and fled to the bathroom. As the scalding water beat on my head, I got myself under control. Dr. Bel said it was natural to shut off parts of my brain in light of what happened to me. True, I'd really only shut off the sex part of my brain, but the thought of the weight of a body pressing down on me made me feel sick and dizzy. Then I thought about the other thing Dr. Bel said; not to make a career of it, because those parts of the brain tend to reassert themselves when you least expect it. Like right now, for instance.

Okay, I told myself. I'm absolutely going to kiss him. I mean, I have to. But that's it. After all, there may be some esoteric rules about interspecies sex that I don't know about. And there was all that stuff about virgins. Christ—what if *he* was a virgin? Seriously, Rube, you're getting a little bit ahead of yourself. Get out there and kiss the gorgeous guy and then say goodnight. Yes, that's the plan. One hundred percent, no wavering.

And, go.

When I came back out, he was sitting on the couch with two opened beers on the coffee table along with several cartons of leftover Chinese takeout he pulled out of the fridge. He was eating tofu drunken noodles, fishing them out of the container with his fingers. Lucky noodles. I sat next to him and went to work on shrimp fried rice. (I used a fork.)

"Can I ask you something?" I took a sip of beer. "Why didn't you want me to touch you?"

He cocked his head, noodles halfway to his mouth. "When did I say that?"

"When I met you. When you were on the ground next to my car, the first thing you said was 'Don't touch me.' But you've touched me since then and nothing happened." I thought about how his hand felt against my neck. Okay, maybe 'nothing' wasn't the right word.

"I have," he agreed. "You're right. I don't really remember saying that. I don't remember much about that night at all, just that you rescued me, and then I was in your car." He looked at the container, and set it down. I handed him a napkin, I don't think I could handle watching him lick his fingers again. "To be honest, I didn't understand what happened right away. I think I must have told you not to come near me because I didn't know I'd been changed. I didn't really get what happened to me until the next morning. If I was in my own body, you definitely couldn't touch me. You saw what that man did to me. But like this? I'm a human man. Nothing special."

"March," I said, "that's not true." He looked so distraught, I wanted to comfort him so much. My plan was starting to evaporate. "Do something for me."

He looked back up at me. "If I can."

"I know you can. Would you put your hand on my neck again? Like you did before?"

He nodded. "Of course. I thought you liked that. Lean back and close your eyes."

I put my food down and rested my head against the back of the couch. I could feel him slide along the cushions until he was next to me. He moved my hair back until my throat was exposed, and placed his palm on the scar. Just like last time, the heat and itch vanished. I heard myself sigh, and I felt him moving against me. His hand went to the back of my head, and I could feel his lips brush my neck. *I am in my body. . .I am alive. . .*and for the first time since the attack, I was.

"Don't cry," he said, touching my cheek. I didn't know I had been. "Do I make you sad?" I leaned forward through the breath of space between us. Instead of speaking, I let him know the answer with a kiss. His mouth was warm and delicious, he tasted like a winter forest, and the forest was on fire and so was I. No one had been this close to me since it happened, and for a minute it was like it never had. He kissed me again, harder, and put his arms around me, we leaned together against the back of the couch. I could feel the weight of him against my chest, and I didn't want to be sitting upright anymore, I wanted him on top of me, I wanted to feel the weight of his body. His hand tangled in my hair and he pulled my head back, and that's when the flames went out and it all came rushing back. The rancid taste of garbage burned my throat, I couldn't breathe; pain flared behind my eyes. *He's not even human, don't let him touch you, you can't get away from him. . .*I pushed him off me and he landed on the floor.

"Oh my god, I am so sorry." I took his hand and helped him back on the couch. We sat quietly for a few minutes. "I haven't. . .you're the first man. . ."

"I'm not really a man, though. Is that part of it?" He reached for his beer and I saw his hand shaking, just like mine. "Would you like me to leave?"

"No, of course not." I forced my breathing to slow down and pulled my robe back so it covered my legs. "You didn't do anything wrong. It's me. I wanted to. . .I still want to. But. . ."

"It's late," he said. "Perhaps you'll feel better after you sleep."

"Maybe you're right." Before I could stand, he leaned over and scooped me up like I was a doll. I caught our reflection in the mirror propped against the wall—his arms cradling me, my arms around his neck, the light shining on his long hair, and then he turned and it was gone.

"Is this okay?" he asked. I nodded, it was very much okay. He carried me to my bedroom and gently sat me on the edge of the bed. "Quiet sleep," he said, "and dream of peace." He kissed me again, a feather brush against my lips, and then he closed the door. I sat like a stone. Well, a stone that was shaking like a leaf. I could hear him moving around, running water, and then the light under the door went out. After another few minutes, I threw my robe over the chair and crawled under the blanket. I took a deep breath and was asleep before I let it out.

6

The next morning, March woke me with a tap on my door. I smelled food and realized I was starving. Once I pulled on some jeans and a hoodie, I went to see what he'd brought home, and from where.

"Ercilia was happy to see me," he said. "She made this for us." He passed me a breakfast burrito and a con leche.

"Does she know this is for me?" I asked.

"Well," he said, "she did say she had a niece she wanted me to meet, so maybe not?" He pointed at a green plastic garbage bag. "She said she went through some old stuff in the thrift store, and that she thinks these will fit. She says she has The Eye." He pulled out another pair of jeans, scuffed motorcycle boots, a couple of t-shirts, and a heavy red plaid flannel shirt. "I'm telling you, she's very nice." He smiled. "She calls me Mister March."

"This is the same woman who yelled at me for taking too

many napkins. But I'm glad you're making friends." I checked the time. "Let's get going."

"To see your mind doctor. Therapist." He looked uneasy. We got in the car and I showed him how to use the seatbelt. I didn't think he cared for being snapped in. "What can she tell me that I don't already know? I have to get used to this body. It's my own fault."

"That's the sort of thing she can help you with. Those kind of thoughts. Blaming yourself." I pulled into traffic on Connecticut Avenue and he gave a huge gasp. I slammed on the brakes and the delivery truck driver behind me gave me a one finger salute. "What? Are you okay? What happened?"

"Nothing. The other car came really close. Is it always like this?" I glanced over and saw white all around his eyes, and he had the armrest in a death grip.

"People in this town drive like maniacs, but fortunately there's so much traffic you can't build up enough speed to do any serious damage. Relax, March. We'll be there in a few minutes." To distract him, and to stop him from gasping with terror every time I went through an intersection, I put the radio on the 70s channel. Whenever he recognized a song, he delightedly announced the fact. I noticed he didn't sing along or move his head or body with the music, he just sat and listened. Maybe unicorns don't have rhythm?

I was starting to pay attention to what he seemed familiar with and what was new. He got in the elevator like he did it every day, but I had to poke him to stop him from staring at a woman in a chador who rode up with us. The office manager, Shanti, said hello and stared at March and handed me the clipboard.

"March, what's your last name?" I got a blank look. He didn't have a last name. Or a social security card, any money, a birth certificate, any ID, or socks. "Never mind. Dr. Bel will help us figure it out."

We got called in right away, and I led him down the soothingly wheat colored hallway lined with impressionist reproductions, and I mentally said hello to the couple in the one painting that was different—it was a hyper realistic oil painting of a woman in an embroidered gown with deep bell sleeves, floor length hair, and a flower crown bending over a forlorn looking knight. I'd noticed it back in Florida and was glad she'd brought it with her.

Dr. Bel rose from her desk chair when we came in, wearing, as always, a charcoal pencil skirt and stack heels that were out of date but looked perfect on her. She was quite stylish for an older lady, I thought.

"Doctor, thanks so much for..." She didn't even glance at me. It was like Claudio all over again, but with shock instead of awe. I turned to introduce March, and got another shock. He was kneeling like he was in front of the pope.

She came out from behind the desk and brushed past me. "Explain yourself, *re'em*. Why do you come before me thusly garbed? After all these years, don't say you come to me now and need my help."

"Madam," he replied, still looking at the carpet between his knees, "I beg forgiveness." He looked up at her. "I did not know it was you."

Now Doctor Bel did look my way, and I guess that was

the moment she realized she couldn't pretend she didn't know him. "Shit," she muttered. "Ruby…" she put a hand to smooth her blonde updo. "Shit. You two had better sit down."

She knew him, or I guess I should say, they knew each other. She was like him. A xeno. I didn't know which was worse, being lied to or wishing I never found out.

Once we were on the couch, she perched on the edge of her desk. "Ruby, I suppose you're wondering—"

"You're one of them, right? So, what are you? An elf or something?"

"Ruby!" It was March's turn to look shocked. "Do you really not know who this is?"

"Up to ten seconds ago I thought this was my human doctor." I glared at her. "Why shouldn't I report you to…the. .."

"It would be the APA, I think," she replied. "Can I try to explain? I understand you feel betrayed…" I shrugged and folded my arms. "When Mrs. Flores contacted me, I already knew who you were. I saw you on the news. I--damn." She pinched the bridge of her nose. "Ruby, do you remember the xeno rights movement? Before you were attacked?"

"Sure," I said. "There was that 'rare but there' thing." Of course I remembered it. I stopped it.

"'Rare but there.' Yes. Well, I came up with that slogan. I was involved. Actually, I was more than involved, I was one of the leaders."

"No way." Was everything she said a lie? My brain instantly turned that into, *'What else did she lie about? The smell, maybe it's still on you after all.'* Shut up, brain.

"I still am, although obviously we don't have much of a movement anymore.

I felt—in fact, I still feel—our kind ought to mainstream. There are so many of us, and we've been here…well, now is not the right time for a speech. And before that, I was—I am—I suppose you'd say important in the xeno community."

"She's a demi-goddess," said March.

"Thank you, March. Anyway, I felt responsible on behalf of our kind for the way you were treated by the press. So public. And the vamps of course were never on board with our assimilation plans, so you could say I bore some responsibility for their more public attacks."

"Like the one on me."

"Exactly. And when you came in, you were in so much pain. I knew I could help you, and I also knew if I told you who I was you'd leave. And after that, it didn't seem pertinent."

"Ha!" I thought March was going to faint at my rudeness.

She glanced at him and he lowered his eyes. A demi-goddess. Maybe she really was the xeno pope? She pursed her lips. "Forget what you've just learned about me. Did I help you?"

"Yes," I snapped. "Obviously. But you still should have told me. So, you're a demi-goddess. What does that make you?"

"It does not 'make her' anything," March said. "She is singular and only herself. She is La Belle Dame."

"La Belle Dame Sans Merci? Like from the poem?" I struggled to recall Freshman English. Something about a woman, beautiful and merciless (it was right there in the title) who was the embodiment of both sex and death, something about a blasted landscape? And now she was standing in front of me. "Sure," I said. "Why not? So why are you a doctor in DC and not roaming a woodland glade seducing knights?"

"Times change," she said. "And so did I. I got tired of pale and forlorn young men trailing around after me. So clingy. I liked modern humans, and I thought they were interesting. I realized I enjoy helping people more than keeping them in my thrall." She gave me a worried look. "You could report me. I mean, I do have a real medical degree. But I technically am a fraud. I lied to you."

I figured at that point I had two choices; I could get up and leave, not look back, and try to forget any of this ever happened. The evidence on my neck made that unlikely. And March--I saved his life, literally picked him up off the street--I was responsible for March. And Dr. Bel was responsible for me. So option two: I could roll with it, and accept the fact that all the monsters in the world weren't necessarily... monstrous.

"Well," I said. "Tell you what. I will keep your secret, but I have one condition."

"Name it," she replied.

"Validate my parking. Forever. Oh, and help March. So, two conditions."

She made a little show out of thinking it over. "You drive a hard bargain. What if I also waive your co-pay for the rest of the millennia?"

"Done." She looked visibly relieved. I was pissed, of course, but I'd be lying if I said I wanted her out of business.

Just imagining not being able to see her made me anxious. "Okay, so how do you two know each other?"

"That human boy broke your heart, that was when I met you," March said. "You were weeping and sighing full sore over that poem he wrote. What was his name?"

"Keats. Thanks for reminding me," she said. "Frankly, I was getting a little tired of watching him compose his great work. Poets." She shook her head. "But then he finished it! Turns out thrall is no match for an adoring public. Anyway, I was wandering near a withered sedge—"

"And no birds sang," he added.

"Of course no birds sang," she said, "it was the middle of fucking winter. Anyway, that's when March and I met." She smiled at the memory. "One minute I thought the moon had come down from the sky. And the next, there you were. You looked just the same as you do now."

"As do you, Madam."

"Stop. I'm wearing an older face now and you know it." I thought she looked pleased.

He shrugged. "You look the same to me."

They admired each other's ageless magnificence for a minute, then March turned to me. "We were companions down through many years. I was sad to leave her side."

"You were not," she said. "You just woke up one morning and said, 'Time to get back to the cold hill's side,' and off you went. It was worse than poetry."

"I missed my body. My real one. And your world is a little too orderly."

"Ah," she said with a smile. "It wasn't me, it was you. Of

course. Well, it's nice to see you after all this time, I suppose. But Ruby, you said he'd been injured. March, what's going on? Why are you in this body?"

I touched his arm. "Tell her what happened."

He went through it, and Dr. Bel didn't interrupt. At one point she went back behind her desk and began taking notes. He might have given me ninja warrior powers I didn't think I actually had, but it was more or less the way I remembered it.

"So you see, Madam, I did this to myself." He had such a look of misery about him, and despite his ageless goddess ex-girlfriend being in the room, I wanted to give him a hug.

"March, please call me Bel, or doctor, or something other than Madam," she said distractedly, still poring over her notes. "Ruby, you said the car had Maryland plates? And one of them—the one you maced—is still alive?"

"They might both be alive," I said. "I didn't check."

"The other man is dead," said March. "Otherwise, I'd be myself and back in my own woods."

"Hmm," said Dr. Bel. "Well, to start, I'll check my contacts at some local hospitals and see if anyone came in with eye injuries. Or if anyone dumped a body at an ER. Next, we should find out who hired that Margaret girl. I have a feeling they aren't finished with you, and we need to find out who and where they are."

"Why did they want to take his horn, anyway? I mean, I've heard they're valuable, and they're obviously magical, but what do they do?" I was a little sorry after I asked, because March looked like he might throw up. I guess it was like asking what good my eyes were, or how someone could use my liver. Gross. But I was still curious.

"Life and death," said Dr. Bel. "Isn't that right?" March nodded. His eyes were closed, tears shone in his long lashes, and even that was beautiful. I was about to take his hand, but looked at Dr. Bel first. She nodded and I did. He gripped my hand tightly.

"I can heal the sick," he said. "I can remedy the poisoned. I can make sour water sweet. I can restore peace to the heart and quiet to the mind."

"And what else?" Dr. Bel asked. I think she already knew.

"I can raise the dead. Once. I can only do that once."

"Have you done it?" I asked.

"Of course not. Why would I?" Then he opened his eyes and looked at me. "Not that it matters now. It's all gone. Because of what I did. You know, that saw wouldn't have worked. It never would. They would have had to take my head, instead. Now my horn is gone and my head is no use to them. Or me. Maybe you should have let them have me."

"Enough of that, *re'em*," Dr. Bel said. "Fate put Ruby in your path, and gave her the bravery to save your life. Then she faced down a vampire, at great personal cost, for fear of them harming you. You think that was an accident? You may be old, older by far than even me, but you don't know what happens next. You both are now part of a story that isn't, I think, even close to being over. Will it be 'happily ever after?' It's not mine—or yours—to know. All we do know is that the tale of the maiden and the unicorn is being written. Did you really want to write yourself out of your own story?"

Looking at her, I couldn't believe I never noticed she was

at least goddess-adjacent. She practically had flames coming out of her head.

March hung his head. "Of course not. I spoke foolishly."

"So," I said, "what does happen next?"

"Well," she replied, "Like I said, they missed once. They will certainly try again. And the vampire girl knows where you live and work. We need a safe place for you both until we get ahead of them."

"But why would they continue? I have nothing they want." March frowned. "Do I?"

"They were denied your horn. They can still get something out of your heart." I wasn't surprised to hear he still had some magic going on, but he didn't seem convinced. Dr. Bel's look softened. "You think you're being punished, locked in this mortal body."

"I am," he replied. "I will be this way forever. I am no longer pure."

"Maybe," she said. "Maybe you're only being educated."

"I don't understand." He looked lost.

"Maybe 'pure' doesn't mean what you think it means. Maybe it's a state one can return to."

"Don't say such things," he said. "Water doesn't flow uphill. Don't give me hope where none exists."

She shook her head. "It is not my intention. And I can't say 'do this, then do that, and you'll be restored.' Yet I am forced to say it is not outside the realm of possibility. But I don't want to make things worse by speculating. Just remember we live in a world where forgiveness is a possibility." He nodded unhappily. I wondered if he believed her. "Let's get back to

Margaret. Who told you to meet her? Who delivered the message?"

He thought about it. "It seems a very long time ago. It was a *kitsune*. He had a message from one of my own kind, one like me who was in need. He said I must make haste to a certain place and I would understand."

Dr. Bel looked amused. "And you trusted a *kitsune*? Never mind. Can you find him again? Was he in your own wood?" He nodded. "Can you find it on a map?" She opened a map program on her desktop, and to my surprise he pointed to the place in the middle of a big green patch on the screen, like he had wifi back home. In a cave. Or where ever. She typed something into her phone, and mine chimed. "This is the GPS to my cabin."

I looked at March, and back at the doctor. "You just happened to have a cabin where he lives."

"No," she said tartly, "I have a cabin I get to use a few time a year several hours away from where he occasionally wanders. Unless you want to sleep in your car, I would say 'thank you'. You should be safe out there, and you can look for this *kitsune*. Keys are under the mat; there's a grocery store two miles before the turn off on West Ridge Road."

"Right. Thank you." I looked at March. I think he was still thinking about purity, and forgiveness. "Ready to take a road trip?"

As we were leaving, Dr. Bel asked if I would stay and talk to her privately. When she was sure March was settled in the waiting room with a copy of Golf Digest, she shut the door and asked me to sit back down.

7

"**I really do forgive you,**" I told her. "Sure, I wish you were more honest, but—hey, is that you, in the painting? With the knight?" Really, how did I not know?

"Yes," she admitted. "But that's not it. I mean, I'm glad you understand, and we can definitely circle back to talk about it when I see you again, but that's not why I asked you to stay." She paused. "This is difficult to explain. I want you to be careful."

"Of vampires? I am. I always carry my spray, and I had the kit under the bed and it worked—"

"Of March."

That stopped me. I made a 'wha?' face, and she continued.

"Ruby, don't fall in love with him."

I just laughed at that. "I literally only met him two days ago."

"And since then, you've devoted every moment to him.

You're about to leave your home to make sure he's safe. Why is that, do you think?"

"Well, I'm responsible for him, aren't I? He doesn't know how to be a person, and how else is he going to get out there to talk to the *kitsune*? He needs me."

She nodded. "He needs help, and you're happy to oblige. Eager, in fact. Have you noticed anyone else who wants to help him? Anyone going out of their way to give him what he wants?"

I had. Of course. I only had to think of Ercilia, and the people at the bar who gave up their seats and sent him drinks. Of poor Claudio, for god's sake. Then I thought of kissing him, of how much I wanted him, and felt kind of sick. "What is it?" I asked. "Some kind of mind control?"

"Not exactly. He genuinely thinks he is without power, that his gifts have been lost, and he's a normal mortal man. We both know he's not. It's like his old glamour is still. . .leaking out, I suppose you could say. I don't even think he knows he's doing it, but I can tell you that before you do something, make sure it's you that wants it, not him wanting you to want it." I nodded. "There's one more thing. He is. . .he's always been powerfully attractive to mortal women Including myself."

"You're a demi-goddess, but you're mortal?"

"I am, as are nearly all of the xeno folk. We count our days in far greater numbers than humans, but we live and eventually we die. March is the exception—his folk aren't mortal; of all the xenos, as you call them, his race are the only truly immortal creatures that exist. He doesn't know how old he is, and he wouldn't understand the need to ask. He doesn't even understand the question. They don't experience time the way we do. Or emotion, or memory, or sacrifice. And I say 'we' because I'm a lot closer in kin to you than to him. I live in a linear world, he doesn't. And one thing I know about every story between a mortal and one of his kind, they always end the same way. He will never fall in love. Not with you, not with anyone, not with anything but his own freedom. I mean, he's an ageless, magical, perfect creature who has no concept of wanting something without getting it. He's never known fear or pain or loss—or the passage of time—until now. That is not a good recipe for mental health—his or yours. You don't have to trust me, and you may think I'm merely jealous because I've been replaced. Perhaps I am. It meant more to me than to him, and it appears time hasn't completely healed my heart. How strange. At any rate, I wish someone would have given me the same warning I'm giving you. I care for you, Ruby, and I don't want to see all our hard work set back. I don't want you to get hurt. Help him, because that's the good person you are, and enjoy him, because it would be foolish of me to tell you not to, but be careful of him."

I stood up. I could feel the heat in my cheeks—that's three times in two days.

"Thank you for telling me. Thank you for the cabin. I'll be in touch." I turned and, well, I didn't run, but I didn't stroll either. I was relieved she didn't follow with more advice. I found March leaning on the receptionist desk, chatting away with Shanti.

"Now you remember to go see Denise—not thin Denise,

East Asian Denise—-she'll give you a decent haircut. Tell her I sent you." Shanti was from Sri Lanka and didn't trust anyone not from that part of the world with hair.

"Shanti thinks I would look better," he told me, "without all of this." He pulled his dark hair into a thumb-length ponytail.

She laughed. "He looks a little VH-1, doesn't he? Tell Denise not to touch that streak, though. People pay good money for something like that."

"What do you think?" he asked me. I didn't reply, only thanked Shanti for keeping him entertained, and after she validated my parking, I headed for the door. He followed. "Is something wrong?"

"Nope," I replied. "Not a thing."

"What did Bel say to you? I feel like something's wrong."

Once on the elevator, I said. "I'm fine. She wanted to remind me to be careful. And we will be, right?" I turned away, pulling my bag across my body. I could feel his beautiful eyes on me. I know he was confused, but so was I. "We have to go back to my place. I need my toothbrush and stuff. And then we can go." I hoped a long car trip would give me time to think. Maybe enough soft rock of the 70's would put him to sleep, so I could.

I called Claudio from the car and made March hold up the phone so I could drive.

"You're on speaker, dude," I said.

"Why are you calling me?" he asked. "Is someone dead?"

"No. . .not yet, anyway. Listen, something's come up, and I need to bounce for a few days. I hate to ask, but can you and

Davy hold down the bar?"

He groaned. "Ugh. Service. Just promise me you're going to go horseback riding—"

"Speaker, Clo." I glanced at March, who was looking out the window at the cars. Maybe he was too nervous to catch the least subtle innuendo of all time. "And don't let anyone know I'm gone. Just act dumb. You can do that, right?"

"Oo, sick burn. Yeah, I'll take care of it. You gonna tell Marly? She'll be pissed if you don't."

I said I would, thanked him, and showed March how to hang up. He spent the rest of the ride playing with the phone and pointedly not looking at the traffic. He must have seen the picture I took of him sleeping, but he didn't mention it.

He waited on the couch while I put together a bag. "Can we bring the bourbon?" he asked.

"I already packed it." I figured by the time we ran out of Makers, it would be time to come home—vamps or not. "You ready?" He said he was, and hoisted the garbage bag full of his newly-acquired stuff. I made a mental note to get him a toothbrush.

I could tell he wanted to ask me what was wrong and why I was avoiding getting too close to him, but instead he helped me hang the garlic and set up the mirror and get the house locked up.

Once in the car, he managed to hook the seatbelt without any assistance. The MINI is small, and our arms were nearly brushing when I had to shift gears. It was like little electric tingles up and down my side.

"Can I have your phone? I want to text Marly," he said.

"Really?" He was full of surprises. Out of the corner of my eye I could see him blazing away. When we got to a light, I looked at what he'd written:

He'd sent her a unicorn and an eggplant, followed by,

Stealing Ruby for a few days don't worry. Will remember what U said

"What did she say?" I asked.

"That if I wasn't nice to you she'd set me on fire. She's a good friend." He paused. "She didn't actually say 'nice.'" I waited. "She said, um, it had to do with the amount of sex I'm supposed to give you." And then it was his turn to blush, and it was fucking adorable. So if I trusted Dr. Bel, I had someone who was so monumentally entitled they didn't even know there was such a thing as 'no.' Like a really, really hot toddler. (That's disgusting, forget I said that.) Like a really, really hot trust fund backpacker you pick up at a youth hostel in Thailand. (I haven't always been in a sex-drought.)

I knew there was no way I'd make it through one night, much less however long it took to find the *kitsune*, without finding out how 'nice' he could be.

8

ince it was mid-week, traffic on 66 was only nightmarish, not a complete shit show. Once we got past Falls Church it even picked up. March figured out that if he closed his eyes when I passed a car, or someone passed me, or I had to hit the brakes, or went into a curve, or basically drove the damned car, it cut down on his anxiety by a lot. Plus I told him I'd pull over and make him walk if he didn't stop gasping. Once we got off 66 and onto 15 there was a lot less traffic, and I think he finally relaxed enough to enjoy the scenery; farms, cows, some estates at the tops of hills that looked like doll houses, and a few times, horses.

"They're pretty, aren't they?" I said. I was curious about his other life, and didn't quite know how to bring it up. I didn't want to hurt his feelings. Horses are unicorn-adjacent, right?

He gave a shrug. "If you like that sort of thing."

"Sure. So. Um, when was the last time you turned into a person? If you don't mind my asking." He knew such a strange mish-mash of current mortal life, I figured it couldn't have been that long ago. Elevators but not cellphones. Therapists but not Kardashians.

"Lots of times," he said. "When I found I was bored, or I wanted to listen to music. Or the company of mortal creatures. Many times."

"But do you know when, like what year? I mean, can you answer that question?" My money was on the late 70s.

"I. . .I know what you mean—my mind knows what you mean, but I didn't think that way before." He looked at me helplessly. "I don't know. I'm different now. In my head." He ran a hand through his hair. "My thoughts are different. One thought right after the other." He was definitely getting torqued.

"It's okay, don't worry about it. I was just curious." I turned up the radio. "Do you know this one?"

"Firefall," he said, and relaxed back into his seat. "Just remember I love you and it'll be all right." He closed his eyes again and listened without moving.

Memory and time, she said. Memory, time and love.

It was just about dark by the time we found the narrow turnoff to Dr. Bel's cabin. I'm glad it was even a little light or else we could have missed it completely. Cell service was spotty and even the GPS came and went. But March spotted the red ribbon tied to a post, and we turned off the main road and were instantly swallowed by the forest. It was so quiet, just the crunching of leaves and twigs under the tires, and the occasional call of what sounded like a hawk.

"It's a blue jay," said March. I figured he probably knew, since this was his home, more or less. He began to cheer up once we got off the highway, and now as the trees closed overhead, he sighed happily. "I was starting to think I'd never see this place again. I know it's only been a few days. . ." he frowned.

I pulled the car into the driveway of the cabin, the only house on the narrow dirt road, and turned off the engine. "What's wrong?"

"A few days. That's what a few days feels like." He shook his head. "It's nothing. Is this it? Can I get out of the car?"

We stretched our legs after the long ride, and took a minute to just look around. The pines met overhead, far above us. It was cool, almost cold, but not late enough in the year for the leaves to be changing, otherwise we'd have seen a lot more people coming out here. As it was, I couldn't even hear the sound of another car.

March carried the groceries we picked up and I took my backpack and his garbage bag of clothes, everything he owned. The key was under the mat next to a pot of mums which bloomed in pink and white. The cabin was small, just one room, but big enough for a dining table and chairs, a lumpy couch, and a small kitchen and even smaller bathroom. And one bed, next to a fireplace. It was immaculately clean.

Since he didn't know how to cook, I let him open beers and keep me company as I worked. I found olive oil and salt in the cupboard, and set some water to boil for the pasta. I realized I wanted to impress him, and I figured that since he wouldn't know a fancy meal from fast food, that desire probably came from my own mind. So I was glad the store had garlic and onions, and late season tomatoes and even basil, and I wouldn't have to pretend pouring a can of sauce into a pot was *haute cuisine*. He watched intently as I chopped and stirred.

"Sorry there were no meatballs," I said.

"Are meatballs made of meat, or are they like sandwiches?"

"Like sandwiches how?"

"No sand, Ruby. They have no sand at all."

I laughed. "Meatballs are made of meat." That made me curious. "Do you eat meat?"

He looked at me like I was about to serve him bird poop or live weasels or something. "Do you?"

"Yes, "I said, "but I won't eat it around you if it bothers you." I thought about the package of bacon in the fridge and kind of regretted making that kind of promise, but you can't take some things back. Anyway, our accidentally vegetarian pasta was a hit. He told me it was the best thing he ever ate, better even that Ercilia's arepas. I think he liked the chocolate ice cream he picked out better than my pasta, but I didn't argue.

After we dumped everything in the sink, we took our bourbons (mine with an ice cube, his neat) and went to sit on the back steps. The cabin was on a ridge, and the hill sloped down dramatically about ten yards past the back door. I set my phone up to stream music, and we had a gorgeous, moonlit view of the mountains in the distance. The grass at our feet was full of fireflies.

"Late in the season for them, isn't it?" I said.

"Is it?"

Maybe they showed up because he wanted them to. Maybe that's why I was here, also.

"I love this song," he said. It was Van Morrison's Into The Mystic. It always reminded me of going out on my dad's fishing boat when I was a kid in Fort Lauderdale. Now it would remind me of March, too.

Again, I watched him simply listen, attentive and still. "Come on," I said. "Get up. Dance with me."

"I don't know how. . .I know what it is, but. . ."

I pulled him to his feet. "It's easy. You don't even have to move your feet." I placed his hands on my waist and put my arms around his neck. I was close enough to catch his pine forest smell and feel the warmth of his body and strength of his back. This is a dangerous idea, I reminded myself. Was this your idea? Is this what you really want? It should have been too dark to see the question in his eyes, but I could see it, and I knew what my answer would be: yes, yes, yes.

I want to rock your gypsy soul. . .

He never did more than hold me close and sway back and forth a bit, but that's all you really need, isn't it?

The fireflies rose and fell around us, a slowly spinning galaxy of pinpoint lights in the velvety darkness.

We were back sitting on the steps.

"What was it like? Living out here for so long? Being a.

. .being what you were." It still felt weird to say it out loud. "A unicorn." I turned to face him. "I'm sorry. I guess you don't want to talk about it."

He shrugged and sipped his drink. "I don't mind. I've been thinking about it. It was different. Time was different. Years would go by, so many years, and I think about it now and all I can remember is there was a beautiful moon one night. Or it snowed that one time. Or I saw a doe with her fawn and traveled with them for a while. Since I met you, since I came into this body, I can't stop my thoughts. I remember everything. Every second. A few days." He shuddered. "It never slows down. I can't figure out what I'm supposed to pay attention to. What's important. How do you have enough room in your heads for all the life that happens to you?"

"We only have a short time, compared to you, I guess. We have to notice everything. And the longer you live as a human, you'll figure out what you need to remember. The rest will fade away." I thought again about what Dr. Bel had said about memory and time. Seemed like she was right about that.

"It's only been a few days, and my old life, my real life, sometimes it seems impossible that I should have lived that way. And sometimes I want to peel off this skin and go home." He pushed his hair out of his face. "But I suppose it'll be over soon." He looked up at me, alarmed, and took my arm. "Really soon. Isn't that right? How long do I have? How many days?"

I put my hand over his. "I don't know. No one does. I don't know if you'll get older, like the rest of us. I guess you probably will. If nothing happens to you, if you don't get sick or hit by a bus or something, you should live until your 80's, maybe? I think that's average." I thought it would make him feel better, that it would seem like a lifetime. A lifetime to me, an eye blink to him.

He put down his empty glass and got up to pace, panic edging into his voice. "That's not long. That's nothing. That's one breath to another. This is my punishment, for what I did to that man. I don't deserve the life I had."

"But that's not fair. You were only defending yourself."

"That's the point." He thumped back down next to me. "My life is of no more value than the man I. . .I killed. I took his life away from him, and so my life was taken from me. It's exactly fair. I picked this path through my own actions, and now I have to accept it. I'm going to die, just like he did." Despite what he said, he didn't look too accepting. "I'm dying right now, aren't I? My skin is going to come off. My hair is going to fall out. I'll get weak. I'm going to die."

I took his hand and held it tight. "March, listen to me, honey. Your skin won't come off. And aging happens so slowly you won't notice it. And you'll have people around you who will love you and care for you no matter how old you are." Of course, I didn't know this for sure. But I had a pretty strong feeling it was going to be true. "Most humans realize they're going to die when they are like, six years old, and it's a lot to take in. None of us know how long we get to live, so we feel like we have forever. Maybe in that way we're a little bit like you were. But soon you'll start to not think about it. And whatever happens, you won't be alone."

He looked at me in dismay. "But how do you stand it? I'm dying."

"No, you're not." I said. "You're living."

I took a second to think about whether I wanted to kiss him right then, or if he wanted me to want to, and I decided both things could be true. So I did. And this time I didn't make him stop or push him away when he wrapped his arms around me, in fact, I held him even tighter. As we kissed, for one disorienting second the ground fell away. He'd lifted me off the steps, and a universe of tiny stars filled the air around us again.

"Take me inside," I said.

There would be time later, I thought, to explore his body and see if it really was perfect, as flawless as a statue, the way it looked when I first found him. I didn't want that now. I pulled his jeans off and made another mental note to get him some boxers. Once our clothes were on the floor, I sat on the edge of the bed and waited to get shy, or nervous, or anxious, but that never happened. When he laid his long and beautiful self out next to me and pulled me down and rolled on top of me, I waited to see if I would panic, but the only thing I wanted was more of him. By the low light of the single lamp, I could see him looking at me, and again I felt a dizzying shift, because he was looking right into me, not thinking of someone or something else, not playing the greatest hits porn reel people use when it's time to perform—he was seeing only me, and letting me know that was perfect.

"You're so beautiful," he said against my ear, "you smell so good."

I kissed him and laughed. "You don't have to keep saying that."

"I'm going to ignore you," he said, and kissed his way down my body. Where his lips touched me was like stars falling, and his hands felt like fire against my skin. "Beautiful mortal girl, fragrant lily, sister of the river, most adored and radiant lady, white and lovely thighs and an unfolding flower between them. . ."

It was the most unconventional dirty talk I'd ever heard, but it got the job done. He kissed away my tears and again told me I was beautiful.

"Now you," I said. If his mouth felt like stars and his hands felt like fire, his cock felt like a shaft of pure light. Like diving in the ocean, but I was floating in bliss. He was, too. And when he was close, he leaned up on his elbows and I watched his face. He closed his eyes and as he came he opened them again, and I suddenly realized I was seeing what he saw; myself, my head against the pillow and my hair fanned out. And you know what? I looked really pretty. He blinked and the image faded away.

I pulled the quilt up over us and we curled up together in the warm bed and looked out the window. I remember the night sky over the mountains being full of shooting stars, but that may have only been in my head.

He placed his palm against my neck, and as before, my skin felt cool and still. "If I was myself I could fix that for you permanently."

I reached down and gently stroked his cock, which jumped against my hand. "You fixed plenty. It was wonderful."

"Mmm." He sounded nearly asleep. "I'm going to try and do what you said," he told me.

"What did I say?" I asked.

"You said I was alive. And that's what I'll do. I'm going to live."

I lay in the dark with my head against his chest and listened to his breath slow to a soft, rumbling snore. I thought about what Dr. Bel told me. 'Don't fall in love,' she said. 'Enjoy him but guard your heart.'

I was starting to think maybe I shouldn't have laughed.

9

I **woke to the pearly light** of not-quite-morning flooding the little cabin, alone in the rumpled bed.

Rolling over, I found March wandering around the small kitchen. He was eating the leftover pasta out of the container (with his fingers, of course) and examining random stuff that was sitting out on the counter. He tasted the olive oil and made a face, sniffed and then sampled the salt, looked curiously at the bottom of the sauce pan, and then lit the burner and stared at the blue and yellow flame, transfixed. While he explored the kitchen, I leaned on my pillow and watched him. He was a sight. I mean, that dimpled ass, that was something I could look at for the rest of my life, no question. I noticed he also had a little softness to his midsection, a bit of a belly, which made a nice contrast with the sharp definition of his hip bones, and his long, powerful legs. I guess that was the result of spending half his time running through the woods, and the other half enjoying mortal food and drink. His chest and stomach were downed with golden brown hair, darker between his legs and fading to nearly blond on his arms, and he had not a bit of a tan line. Even the thick curve of his penis was tan. He looked over his shoulder and caught me watching him.

"Are you going to stare or are you going to show me how to make coffee?"

"Neither," I said. "Get back over here." He did, and I did what I'd been wanting to do since we shared our first meal; I licked his fingers.

"What a pleasure you are, my mortal flower, my shiny stone."

I laughed. "Did you just call me a rock?"

He smiled and kissed my wrist. "Rocks are very important. I like rocks. They're smooth," he moved to the crook of my elbow, "and they're strong," and on to my breasts, "and they feel good under your hand when you touch them." Satisfied that he'd made his point, he flipped me onto my stomach. I felt his lips on the back on my neck. The warm weight of him was comforting, not confining. His hands went under me and he found the right place to touch, and I lifted my hips so he could go harder against me. Instead he pulled his hands back so his touch was light as a feather, which was sheer torture. After a while I think I just about blacked out from lust and begged him for more. He sat up and pulled me backwards by the ankles onto his lap, and I'm glad there were no neighbors because I cried out when he parted my legs and went inside me. I gripped the headboard and pushed back against him and he made the very same sound. He leaned forward and kissed the back of my neck again, and then he ran his fingers down the center of my back, along my spine, and it was like I was unzipped. No, that's not right. I was unfolded, just like the pages of a book. He opened me up, exposed every nerve ending, and everything I felt, from his mouth, from his hands, from his body, where we were joined together, I felt not only in my own sex, but in every cell. I felt like a bell, ringing and ringing. Each of his thrusts went through me like a breaking wave, reaching my fingertips and surging back to crash against him. And when we got to our moment together, I opened my eyes and saw not just myself, like last time, but both of us. I could only glimpse us in a scribble of faint lines, we were surrounded by color and light—white and rose and gold, pulsing and writhing with every heartbeat, floating a foot or so above the bed. Eventually the color and light faded away.

A while later, I rolled onto my side. "What *was* that?"

He had the nerve to look concerned. "Was it not good for you?"

"Ha, right. Okay. Seriously, what just happened?"

He leaned back and smiled. "You know how everything has a vibration? Not just sentient creatures, but everything." He lifted my hand from where it rested on his chest, and brought it to his lips. I got a residual tingle. "Every stick of wood, every fish, every drop of water. Even a shiny stone. Everything. When they are played together in the right combination, something wonderful can happen."

"You were playing me?"

"We vibrated together. We struck a chord."

I could sort of see that. It was like music, made of light. "Huh. You really are something."

"Yes," he agreed. "But what?"

It was much later in the morning when we finally got showered and coffeed up and dressed. I gave up on forks and made us toast and eggs, no utensils required, and made up a couple of sandwiches from the leftovers. After we ate, I unfolded the map we got at the grocery store, and spread it out on the table. He stood and walked around it, occasionally leaning in to take a closer look. I think he might have been slightly nearsighted.

"We are here," he told me, "and we need to go here." The two points he'd marked in pencil were a little more than an inch apart, and I loaded the place he wanted to go into the GPS. Even if we lost the satellite, I thought I could find it. It was on Skyline Drive near the Loft Mountain Overlook.

"I want to learn how to drive," he said, watching me steer the car through the twisting mountain roads. "I want a phone. And a stove." He looked worried. "I have a lot to do if I'm going to live. Will you help me?"

"Of course," I said. "Whatever you need." I thought about jobs and taxes and houses and money. "You have plenty of time."

I parked at the scenic overlook, and we got out and I let him take a couple of pictures with my phone. It was quiet out there, and cool, and so beautiful I could see why he'd made it his home. "I've never been here before," I said.

"I may never come here again," he replied, handing it back.

"You okay?"

He shrugged. "It's different now. It looks different." He rubbed the back of his neck. "I want to see it as I always did, but it's like I can't stop thinking about what I want to do next." I made yet another mental note to introduce him to yoga if we didn't get beheaded or eaten by vampires.

We walked on for another hour or so, and every so often he'd stop and introduce me to a tree he was acquainted with, or point out a bird he knew. We stopped a few times for water breaks, and I let him eat the sandwiches. I was still feeling floaty and relaxed from the morning's activities, and wasn't hungry. Marly called it sex-brain, and I had it bad.

We were following a narrow trail that looked just like every other one we'd hiked, mossy rocks and ferns in the path, pines far above, when he stopped short in front of me. He held a finger to his lips and pointed at a tree about twenty yards ahead of us. Sleeping at the foot, curled up in the shrubby weeds, was a red fox the size of a Great Dane. Near its pointed black muzzle sat a white ball, like a softball. At first I thought it was just painted a really bright color. Then I realized it was glowing.

"Go around behind him," March whispered in my ear. "I'll talk to him, and you pick up the ball. He'll do anything to get it back. He'll tell us who hired him."

Feeling very Mission Impossible, I crept into place behind a curtain of trees and bushes, and waited to see what would happen. March rolled up on the fox like he was transit police and the animal had slept through its bus stop and nudged it with the toe of his boot.

"Wake up, Brother," he said. "And let's have a talk."

I could see the fox sit up and yawn, and then it was like he strobed for a second, and a skinny red-haired naked man sat on the ground instead. He had a sharp, zoo smell. "This is a surprise," said the fox. He, like March, had a silky voice, but there was something a little staged about the way he spoke. He sounded like a radio announcer. "Why are you wearing that man suit? And so many clothes." The man sniffed. "Ah, you've been keeping company, I gather."

Gross.

"Why is this a surprise, *kitsune*? Wasn't I supposed to find my friend and come back home? One would think you'd be looking for a reward." He stepped back from the fox man, so that if the *kitsune* wanted to continue talking he'd have to turn away from his glowing ball. The man stood and stretched and took a step away from it. I always thought fox spirits were supposed to be sexy, but this guy was dirty, stringy and smelly. He still hadn't looked back at the ball. I figured one more step and I could grab it.

"Ah well, the city is a wild and dangerous place, even for one such as yourself." The kitsune looked around. "But where is she? Did you not find her there in the world of men?" She? That got my attention, but so did the next two or three paces he took away from his spot by the tree. I made my move.

"Got it," I said. March smiled at me, and the fox man whirled and hissed. He showed me his pointed teeth, which were as yellow as his eyes.

"Explain yourself, *re'em*. Why have you brought a mortal here? Other than to fuck, I mean."

"Rude," I said. I edged around the *furious* kitsune and stood behind March. The ball was cool and smooth and I tossed it from hand to hand. "What is this?" I asked.

"Nothing of value to you," the fox man said. "Give it back at once." He held his hand over his heart. "I'll die without it. Did he tell you that? I already sicken. . ."

"Ignore him. It's the seat of his power. It would hold his soul, if he had one, which he doesn't."

"Yes I do," said the kitsune. "Anger has made you a liar." He looked back at me and made a sad face. "Please help me, mortal girl."

"Be quiet. He's useless without it, nothing more than a helpless mortal man with no clothes and no friends." I hoped the *kitsune* couldn't tell the truth of March's own condition. Dr. Bel would have called it transference. "She'll give it back when you give us an answer," March continued. "And it's an easy question. Who told you to give me that message? Who wanted me in the city that night?"

"Ah," the *kitsune* said. "Then you didn't find Gaia. Too bad. You were so excited." He glanced at me. "You've traded down, *re'em*. This one isn't even her shadow."

"Gaia wasn't there, don't act like you thought that was true." He turned to me. "Listen to nothing this creature says."

I wanted to ask who Gaia was, and I also didn't want to know.

"You should have seen yourself, though. At the mention of her name, I could see it in your eyes." He was talking to March, but looking at me as he spoke. "A chance to go after Gaia the Fair, Gaia the Magnificent, she of the White Feet, sister of the—"

"Sister of the river," I said. I'd heard that phrase before, and recently. "Who is Gaia?"

The foxman laughed. "Who indeed. Strange that he didn't tell you, since he'd move the world to find her. He put himself in the most deadly danger, just on the off chance that I was right. He knew not to trust me, and yet he couldn't stay away. And you, he got you to help him, oh and I bet you were so helpful."

"Gaia isn't here." March snapped. "She has nothing to do with this. Who sent you to me?"

Instead of answering, the foxman fixed his attention on me. "What have you done for him, mortal girl? Are you special to him? Has he used you in ways most riveting and peculiar? What wouldn't you do for him now? He's got you stealing and blackailing, hasn't he? What else?"

"Blackmailing," I said, "I think you mean. Tell us who hired you and you can have your thing back." I was feeling sort of queasy by this point—sex brain having vanished—and I wanted to go back to the car. I wanted to go home.

The fox man sighed. "Fine. It was Barbara."

We glanced at each other. "Did you say Barbara?" I said.

"Mm Hm. Barbara. . .Yeager. Yes, that's it. I'm certain

of it. Now, back to Gaia. Oh, you should have seen her. And the two of them together, what a sight. Although with mortal eyes her loveliness may have been too much for you. How nice, though, that your friend here has found a plaything to keep him occupied until he does find her."

"Are we done?" I asked March. He shrugged. I put the ball on the ground and rolled it in the *kitsune's* direction. He leapt on it and strobed again, turning back into an enormous fox. With a nasty laugh, he flipped the ball into a curl in his tail and vanished into the woods. We were alone.

10

"Who is she?" I asked again. I'd been walking behind March for an hour, mostly in silence, but the longer I was quiet the more upset I got. The worst part was, I wasn't even sure if I had the right to be angry. On the one hand, I had a fling with a handsome stranger. He wasn't obligated to tell me about all the random hookups he'd had before we met two days ago. On the other, this had been a pretty intense couple of days, and he wasn't your typical handsome stranger. And I didn't get the impression this Gaia was a random hookup. Far from it. But when I asked about her, he either wouldn't or couldn't reply. I wasn't sure if he was being evasive, or if it just didn't make sense to his new, mortal mind. "You were looking for her. So who is she? Your girlfriend? Your wife?"

"I can't explain, Ruby. I don't think you'd understand. I don't think I do."

"Try me, because to me right now it looks like Dr. Bel was right about you."

He stopped and turned. "Bel said something about me? What was it?"

"She said you make people do things, that you have no concept of love or loyalty. That you always have to get your way, no matter what."

Rather than getting angry, he looked disappointed. "She said that about me? Do you believe her? Do you think I made you do anything?"

"I don't know." I crossed my arms over my chest. "Maybe."

He gave a strangled laugh. "Better you should have let those people take my life than think I forced you to take me to your bed. That's what you're talking about, isn't it?" I didn't answer. "Tell me, if I'm so powerful, why aren't you happy and trotting along behind me right now? Surely you don't think I want to make you angry."

"Tell me who she is. Tell me you aren't using me for fun until you get her back."

Now he looked confused. "Is it wrong to have fun? Did you not enjoy what we did together?"

"Don't change the subject." I started walking again, probably in the right direction. "It didn't even occur to you that the *kitsune* would mention her, and I would hear it. Or that is would upset me."

"Why should it? She has nothing to do with you. She's not here."

"I know she's not here. Just tell me who Gaia is."

"She is one like myself," he said. "And my companion

since time was young. And now she's gone."

I stopped again, and turned to face him. "Was that so hard? And the *kitsune* knew—or this Barbara person, I guess—knew that dropping her name would bring you to them. How long has she been gone?"

"I don't know," he said wearily. "Look, there's the car."

We packed the cabin up and got back on the road without speaking, deciding without discussing it that it was time to go home. Every time I looked at him, I could feel a rush of warmth, and I wanted to tell him to forget it, I still want you, let's go back to the way it was this morning. But as much as I wrestled with asking myself if I really felt that way, I didn't have an answer.

The ride back to DC was tense, even though March either pretended to or actually did fall asleep, so we didn't have to tack another two hours onto our argument. All the way home I listened to the 80's channel; spiky synths and drum machines. I knew Margaret and her crowd were still out there, but I also figured if March wasn't with me, we might both be safer. Well, that's not entirely right. I thought I would be safer if he were somewhere else, at least until I could figure out what I was feeling other than guilty and angry; guilty for wanting to get away from him when he had no one else, and angry for being used. Happily, joyfully used. I had a plan that involved dumping him on Dr. Bel and then getting out of town for a few days. I had some friends in Boston I hadn't seen for a while.

I sat in the car in my driveway for a few minutes, trying not to watch him sleeping, trying not to abandon my plan and forget what the *kitsune* said. From the driver's seat, everything looked quiet. I figured I'd get inside and call Dr. Bel and let her know we were back and what we found out. I'd save Gaia for when I saw her. I had a feeling she'd have something to say other than 'I told you so.'

Finally, I poked him in the shoulder. "We're here."

He blinked awake, and reached for me, smiling. "Good morning. Oh, I guess it's late."

I smacked his hand. "Did you literally forget we were fighting? You did, damn it." I got out and slammed my door. "I have to make some calls."

"I don't understand why you are angry," he said, and for the first time, he sounded angry too. "I told you who she was. She's not here. What's the difference between us?"

I paused at the door. "So you're telling me Gaia is gone?"

"She's gone." Then he looked puzzled. "Isn't she?" I threw up my hands and he continued. "Ruby, why are you being this way? You know what I am."

"I know what you were." Well, that one landed, and I felt awful. I sounded as spiteful as the fox. But before I could try and apologize, he backed away.

"I'm going. . .I want to. . ." he turned and walked rapidly down the alley.

"Shit." I went inside with our bags and my backpack, and put everything on the floor by the door. I pulled out my phone and plugged it into the charger on the kitchen table. I figured I'd get the beer and whatnot put away and then call

Dr. Bel. Hopefully by then March would have come back from wherever he went. I hoped he came back soon, but I realized I wouldn't be completely surprised if he never came back at all. He had no ties to me beyond a couple of 'fun' nights. I was so shitty to him my rescue probably didn't seem as noble anymore, and I knew his heart was with someone else. Maybe he'd go looking for her, and I would never see him again.

"Aww, did you get in a fight with My Little Pony? That's sad."

I whirled. "Jeez, Marly, hide in the dark much? And that was a crappy thing to say." I turned the light on. "What are you doing here? Is everything okay?"

"Waiting for you. And him," she said. "Just waiting." Then she got up off the couch and came into the light. Her blouse was ripped and had dark stains around the neckline, and her eyes were flat and shiny.

"Oh no. Oh, Marly." I backed away, trying to remember where I packed my spray. "Oh my god, what happened?"

She laughed. "I think you know." She pantomimed fangs in her neck with two curved fingers. "So, where's the horse, Ruby? You didn't let him gallop away, did you?"

"He's gone," I said. "Never coming back. Marly, I'm so sorry. How. . .who. . .." It was hard to speak but I had to ask. Then I got a horrible thought. "Is Claudio. . ."

"Wouldn't you like to know," she smirked. "Ah, I can't lie to you, he's still alive. We looked for him, though. Maybe we'll find him soon."

"Who did this? Why?"

"Well, first, some basic bitch came around and wanted your keys. We had a beer and I told her to fuck right off. So she sent some vamp girl—didn't catch her name. She said she was turning me for you, so you'll know they're serious. Hey, I'm a gift!"

"Oh my god, I'm so sorry..."Tears blurred my vision, but I could see the neat bite marks on her neck well enough. The vamp girl had been telling the truth, she had set out to turn Marly, not kill her. Otherwise her neck would have looked like mine.

"And once that was taken care of, blonde bitch and her boys came and cleaned all your nasty garlic and threw it in the dumpster." She leaned closer and for the first time, I got a whiff of her. "They wanted me to sit in the dark and wait for you so you wouldn't run away. They needed me like this. And I'm so glad they did it. . .."

My skin crawled like I was talking to a spider, but I had to try and reach her. "I know you still remember what being alive felt like." She cocked her head and looked at me, curious. She was in there, I knew it. "But soon you won't. Can you feel it? You're fading away. Try to remember being alive, can you do that? Because if you don't it'll all be gone."

"I know. And I can't wait." She grinned and for the first time I saw her new little fangs. Her gums were grey; dirty looking fluid wept from the wounds the teeth made in her lower lip and ran down her chin.

I swallowed hard. "Marly, you know I love you, right?"

She smiled, and for one fleeting, final second I could see my friend inside that rotting shell. "I love you too!" she said.

"And once I eat you, if there's anything left you can be just like me. It feels so good. . ."

"Marly, I love you. It's important that you know that, but I swear to god I'll cut your heart out before I let you touch me."

She laughed, shrill and long, and my friend was gone.

By now it was dark enough for her to throw my back door open. "Oh look! Some awful people are here to see you," she said. Margaret and the two men still alive from the other night strolled into my house like they owned it. One of them had a white plastic patch taped over his eye. Good.

The men pushed me onto the couch and zip tied my hands and ankles together. *I am alive, I am in my body. . .* The problem with mantras against triggers is that they don't really help when you're in actual danger. I prayed that March would come back, and also that he was miles away.

Smiling like a beauty pageant contestant, Margaret came over and slapped me across the face. "That's for ruining a perfect set up. And for Bobby."

"He's the dead one," said Marly. The three looked at her. "I'm just trying to be helpful. God, you people. Ugh, if you won't let me eat her I am outtie. This is so boring." Without another word or glance at me, she sauntered out the back door and vanished.

"Where's the horse?" asked Margaret.

"Have you tried the stables at Rock Creek? I know all the police horses are there—" She whacked me again, with a closed fist this time. My head rang and I could feel the tingling itch of a black eye starting. The lights got hazy shimmering haloes around them. I can't explain why I was being snarky, I'm not brave and I'm not clever. I felt like I was watching a movie. One I wanted to turn off.

"Where's your friend?" she said.

"She just left." She hit me again, in the mouth this time, and I spit blood onto her blouse.

"Fucking fuck!" She leapt back. "Michael, see if this cow has seltzer in the fridge. Blood is a bitch to get out." To me she said, "Well, this has been fun, but we need to get you on the road. The boss wants to see you."

"Oh," I said, "you mean Barbara?"

She looked at me like I was the crazy one. "Sure. Whatever. Barbara, I get it." She laughed. "The horse will come looking for you. I'm surprised he hasn't shown up already." She picked up my phone and after futzing with it for a few minutes, she held it up and pointed the back at me. "Time for a hostage video! Ready for your close up?"

"Why are you doing this? Just leave, I won't tell anyone."

She stared at me. "My daddy always said the dirty ones have the shiniest words. Your friend, the horse. He's a killer. He has to pay."

"But...but he didn't do anything until you attacked him."

"I should listen to you? You're not only a fornicator, you lie down with animals. You're disgusting."

"He's not an animal." Tears joined the blood on my face. My neck itched so badly I could barely stand it. "He's gone. I don't know where. I can't help you."

"Sure you can." She pushed the record button. "Repeat after me. If you want to see me alive, come to Chicago."

"March, don't listen, don't go—" That got me another whack. My head spun, I couldn't focus. I repeated what she said.

"Good. Now say, 'I'm in Millennium Park, and I miss my horsie soo bad.'"

"Millennium Park? You mean near the lake?"

"That's enough, I guess." She tossed the phone onto the kitchen table. "If no one finds it, your vamp friend Marly gets to show you the ropes in a few days."

"Why did you have to turn Marly? She has nothing to do with this. What's wrong with you people?"

"We had to promise her something for giving up your keys. Even after we turned her, she wouldn't let us have them. And you're such a paranoid bitch you'd have spotted a broken window or something. Also, I felt like it." She signaled the two men who lifted me right off the couch. "Anyway, let's hit it. For your sake, you better hope the horse comes back to his barn."

One of the men went around behind me, and I felt a cold sting in my arm. When I opened my eyes again, there was nothing to see.

11

I **woke up and threw up** almost at the same time.

When I realized my hands were free, I wiped my face on my shirt tail and slowly pulled myself upright. I was in a truck, either a small U-Haul or a panel van—the kind without windows, and without the tail lights that you're supposed to kick out if you get kidnapped on TV. It was almost completely empty. Over my head was a small grilled square that let some night air in, along with a band of orange sodium lights every few seconds. I could hear trucks and we didn't stop, so we were on an interstate, probably heading for Chicago. The cab was separate from the back part, and if I pressed my head against the front wall, I could barely hear the bass line of the radio. Whatever they knocked me out with was just about worn off, and I took deep breaths of diesel scented air to clear my head.

My hands were free, but my ankle were still looped

together, and the plastic ties were way tougher than my fingernails, or even my teeth.

I tried to get a handgrip on the grate in the roof to look out, or maybe even stick my fingers up to. . .I don't know, wiggle for help? But my tied feet made it impossible to stand up straight, and the holes in the grate were too small, anyway. I wondered how far north we were, and what would be waiting for me when we got to Chicago.

I thought about the sandwiches I'd let March eat, and my stomach rumbled painfully. I wondered where he was, and if he—or anyone—would see the video on my phone.

It would have been better if I woke up half an hour outside of Illinois, but instead I had that night and half of another day to lay on my side and think about how hungry I was. And once I started to feel like I had to pee, everything else took a back seat, although 'thirsty' gave it a good run for its money. Finally, having to pee won, and that was another level of disgusting. At first I hoped someone would have called the police and told them I was missing, but then I remembered I'd let Claudio know I'd be gone for a few days, and I never got to call Dr. Bel to let her know we'd cut our trip short. God, that was a stupid move. That fox man should have been a lawyer, the way he played me. It was like I wanted to get snatched.

And always in the back of my mind, Marly. And March.

Finally, the truck pulled to a stop. I crawled to the far front of the cab and waited. One of the guys swung the door to the truck open, and he made a face at the pee-smelling air. I tried to kick him when he pulled me out by my feet. He cut the straps on my ankles and set me down and I fell over. The two men looked at each other, disgusted, and pulled me back up. We were in a huge parking garage, and I spotted a couple of touristy looking people bundled in their puffy coats searching for their cars.

"You should yell for help," said Margaret, who leaned casually against the hood of the car parked next to us. You could tell she practiced her poses. She took off her sunglasses and polished them on her scarf. "Call to them. Or run. I want you to see what would happen."

I ducked my head. I didn't want anyone else to get in trouble because of me. The two guys each took me by an elbow and held me up, and we walked out into a late afternoon on East Washington Street in Chicago. Loads of people rushed past us, no one even looked in our direction. We headed for the lake.

When people think about Millennium Park, they usually think of the Bean, the big silver sculpture. But there are lots of other things there, things you could hide in. Things you could live in, if you had the right kind of xeno powers. That's where they took me. It was one of the giant heads. I was so hungry and sore from rolling around the back of the van, all I could do was try and not get dragged, so I couldn't tell you which one. But Margaret did something or said something, and the back of the sculpture turned to smoke. They hauled me in.

I was getting the feeling back in my legs by this point, and I was starting to feel less scared and more angry. Or maybe it was so unreal I didn't know how to feel about it. The sculpture of the head was pretty big, but no way could it hide a room this size. One second I was feeling the cold breeze off the lake, and the next I was in a damp, windowless, torch lit hut. I mean, it was a really big space, but when I see a dirt floor with a kettle or cauldron or whatever hanging in a huge fireplace, I'm thinking hut.

Margaret pointed at a plain metal folding chair in the middle of the room, and the guys pushed me into it. They pulled out another set of zip ties. "Oh, come on. I won't go anywhere. I can hardly walk."

"I know," said Margaret. "I don't care."

"What turned you into such a raging bitch? Is it the lack of D?"

She watched the two men tie me to the chair, with my arms down at my sides. "What about you? I took a look around your sad little house after we changed your friend." She smiled sweetly. "Honestly, I think we gave her an upgrade."

I lurched forward in the chair, knowing it was useless. "I'm going to kill you for that."

"Heh. Sure you are. Anyway, yeah. Went through your stuff. And I noticed something."

"Good for you."

"No pictures. I was curious where such a nosy, nasty, ugly person could come from, so I looked around. Where's mom and dad? Old boyfriends? Dead pets? There was nothing on your fridge but takeout menus. Sad. So then I looked for anything personal. Know what I found? Nothing. Not even a plant. A lot of medical records, though. Those were interesting." She tilted her head and took a delicate sniff.

"You were right all along, you do stink. That was when I knew we could get you here with no trouble. No one cares about you. No one will miss you. Those vamps in Florida should have finished you off and saved everyone a lot of trouble."

"I'm really sorry you had such an unhappy childhood," I told her. She glared at me. "I mean, for you to turn out this way. I'm sorry that Child Services missed your house. I bet I know who decided you ought to be a professional virgin. Hey, does that gig come with dental?" One of the men snickered. "So, I guess your daddy was a big-time child toucher, huh?"

"You shut up," she hissed.

I had no idea about her father, but she'd mentioned him and called him 'Daddy' which felt like a red flag. I think Dr. Bel would have agreed. Why did I want to piss her off so much? Probably the same reason she zipped the ties on my wrists tight enough to make my fingers tingle. Some people you just don't like.

"I mean, if he put it in your ass, technically you're still a virgin, right?"

She leaned over me, and I could smell her shampoo— fresh and sweet. She yanked the ties tighter; my hands began to go numb. "*Technically* one of us is tied to a chair, and one is heading out for a beer and a burger. Mmmmm, that'll be good! Can I bring you back anything? No?" She wiped her hands on her jeans, like I was slimy. Maybe I was. "Okay," she said. "We're done here." She led the men off into the shadows at the opposite end of the room. I was alone.

I guess I told her, though. Right?

My hands were turning purple and I was trying not to think about how thirsty I was. Being hungry—for real hungry, not skip a meal because I overslept hungry—felt like a fist in my stomach and I could try to ignore it, but the thirst was constant; my tongue was dry and furry as an old rug and it stuck to the roof of my mouth. *I am alive*, I reminded myself, but I had to add *for now*. I tried to inventory the room for something to do, to keep the panic away. I was in a little dome of light cast by the fire in the giant fireplace. The flame was a sort of grayish-green, and it burned my eyes to look right at it. There was enough light to see that the rough wooden table would have come up to my chin, and on it stood a concrete-looking grey stone mortar and pestle about a foot tall, a knife as long as my arm, and a couple of plus-sized wooden bowls and plates. I tried to see the ceiling, but it was all shadows. I could make out sheaves of what looked like wheat hanging in the murk, maybe hanging to dry? I looked up at them, wheat and something smaller and darker. When I realized they were strings of dead mice and birds, I looked away. The packed dirt floor was just as strange, marked everywhere with long, deep gouges. *They'll never pick this place on House Hunters*, I thought, and gave a stupid laugh. I could hear rustling and thumping noises just out of the limit of the firelight, and once I heard something cough. Maybe it was a laugh, I don't know. I thought I could hear owls hooting outside. Is that possible? Are there owls in Chicago? I couldn't see what was in the pot over the fire, but something was simmering. It had a metallic, greasy odor. One more smell to wash out of my hair, if I somehow survived this. I imagined standing in the shower and letting the fresh, beautiful water run over my face and down my throat. . .and then there was water on my lips. It was real and it felt like heaven. I opened my eyes and that was like heaven, too. But it was all wrong.

"March, get out of here," I whispered, but only a dry rasp came out. He held the water bottle up and I drank, too fast. He patiently waited for me to stop coughing, and held it up again. When I could swallow without it hurting, I repeated, "You have to get out of here. You know what they want."

"Yes," he agreed, gently wiping water drops off my face. "Are we still fighting?"

"No," I gasped. "I guess not. But you shouldn't have come here. You have to leave."

"I thought a lot about what you said," he told me. "Here, drink some more. About not knowing how many days you have, not being able to count them, and how that made my kind a little more like your kind. You can't count the future, I can't count the past. But you mortals can decide about the future, can't you? That's something I would never think to do. Maybe being able to decide how many days you have makes your kind special. Maybe that's what Bel meant when she said I was being educated. Maybe even if you aren't pure, you're still worth saving." He set the water bottle on the floor, stood up and addressed the darkness. "Anyway, Madam, I'm here. As you requested."

Again, that gagging, coughing noise. I think it was a laugh after all.

"Who are you talking to? Who's Madam?" I struggled against the ties, but it only made them bite my wrists more deeply.

Instead of answering, March continued to talk to the dark room. "Before we continue, I need your assurance that the mortal woman's part in this is done."

"I said so, didn't I?" Out of the murk came a bent-backed little old lady. But she wasn't little. She was about nine feet tall, if she straightened up it might have been closer to twelve. She had a grotesquely warty, oversized nose, like a for-real cartoon witch, and she walked as if her feet hurt her. Now I understood the tall table and the giant cutlery. She snorted loudly, spat into the fire, and then pulled a tablecloth out of her pocket and blew her nose. "Since when is it necessary for me to repeat myself? A deal's a deal. Heh." She swung her huge head in my direction. "Oh, dear. What did that nasty old Margaret do to you? I must talk to her about how to treat guests. Not her fault, really. The way she was raised, you know." She lifted a gnarled hand the size of a manhole cover and waved it at me, and the zip ties turned to pasta—cooked pasta. "If I told that girl once, I've told her twice. She knows I can't abide those things. Plastic," she shook her head. "Not in my house." I yanked my hands up and the noodles fell on the dirt floor. I confess, I was so hungry I actually considered eating them. Didn't, though.

"Thank you," I said to her, rubbing my red, swollen hands and flexing my puffy fingers. I figured I might as well be polite to the giant magical grandma. "Are you Barbara Yeager?"

She stared at me like Margaret had for a second, and

then cackled, which turned into more gagging and spitting. "Close enough, dearie. Well, we can't have you interfering a second time, can we? Let's take care of that." I tried to stand, but the pasta turned into roses, the vines twisted themselves around my ankles and up the insides of my pants legs, and I couldn't move. I could see bloody dots spreading on my jeans from the thorns. Huge, deep red blooms poked out from around my ankles. "Aren't they pretty? I know how much you humans like pretty things." And then she said to March, "Speaking of. She'll be released when our work here is done. Let's get on with it."

"Get on with what?" I asked March. I mean, I knew. I saw the knife. I knew.

"He's here to right a wrong, among other things," she said. "And to honor a bargain."

"Yes," he agreed. "I am." Then he turned to me. "I tried, but I didn't know how hard it would be. I didn't understand how hard it is to live like you do. To count the days. I didn't understand that creatures who were not myself were really real. Maybe if it was for any other reason, I'd keep trying, to learn how to live in this world. But this makes it easy to decide. That it's not all for her," and here he nodded at the old lady, who pulled a face like she was offended. "It's for you."

"What's hard?" I asked. "What do you mean? What's for me?" As long as I was asking stupid questions, no one was picking that knife up off the table.

"He means being in that pretty mortal body is too much work, and he isn't enjoying his punishment. Look at it this way, I gave him an easy way out. His life for yours."

"It's fine," he told me. "It all makes sense."

"It certainly does," Barbara agreed. She hobbled to her wooden table, and her long skirts swished. At first I thought she was wearing yellow boots, but she wasn't. She had giant chicken feet, her long, dirty claws were what scored the floor. No wonder she had trouble walking. I wondered if she could run. "It could have gone either way—I would have had the horn, or the head, and that would have been best. But since he took a life, he knows that his own is forfeit. So here he is, willingly giving up his heart. That will do for now."

"For what?" I shouted. "Why?"

"Why, to save my own life, of course." She was smiling kindly at us, like she was talking about knitting an afghan, not murder. "Unlike your friend here, I don't get to live forever. He can help with that. His heart won't be as good as his horn, but like I said, it'll do."

March leaned down and kissed my cheek. "Don't cry, little stone. I got to pick my day."

"Don't do this, please, let's run, she's sick, she can't catch us, let's get out of here. . ."

"If he does that, human girl, it will only be to please you. He wants to be pure again, and he can't do that while he's wearing a human body. Lucky for him I came along, really."

"Wait," I said, "You can make him pure? The way he was?" I was still stalling, but what if it were true?

She laughed. "For him, the only path back to purity is death."

He went to meet the old lady in the middle of that dark, cold space, and stood in front of her. She got the huge knife off the table. "Thank you for this, *re'em*," she said, licking her thumb and running it along the blade. "You've made an old lady very happy. And considerably less old." He closed his eyes and tilted his head back, opening his arms. I wanted to close my own eyes, but I didn't. I owed him that much, right? So I watched as she raised the knife, and I watched as she lowered it towards the center of his chest. I watched as the light in the room started to grow, until I couldn't see him anymore because it was as bright as the sun, and then the sun, the stars, all the light in the world, it all exploded at once.

12

"**I**s she drunk?"

"I bet she's on drugs. Look at her hands—probably a sex thing that went bad."

"Honey, can you hear me?"

"Should I call 9-1-1?"

I blinked a couple of times at the blue sky over my head. A circle of concerned-looking people standing over me came into focus. I seemed to be lying on the grass, and my hands and feet were free. No pasta, no roses. The late sun was bright, and the wind off the lake was cold. The smell of dirt and damp lingered in my nose. And another smell, like ozone. That was when I remembered, and I shut my eyes tight.

"Let me through, please, I'm her doctor." I opened my eyes a crack, and sure enough, Doctor Bel was kneeling next to me, with Shanti leaning over her shoulder. Dr. Bel kept her face locked up, but Shanti looked shocked and had her hand over her mouth. "Can you sit up?" I could. "She's my patient," she explained. "We thought she was ready for a day out, but she slipped away from us. Come on, dear, let's get you inside."

"Is she going to be okay?" Most of the people around me were relieved they didn't have to get involved. "What happened to her?"

"She was in an accident," said Dr. Bel, "and there was some traumatic injury. This is part of her reintegration. She'll be fine. No, we don't need 9-1-1. Thank you all, you're very kind. I've got her now." The last few bystanders wandered off. "Ruby, honey, can you walk? I have a car right around the corner."

The two of them helped me back to their rental. Shanti handed me a water bottle from her purse. "As soon as we figured out where they took you, I had Shanti get us a room close by. We just now saw all those people standing around. . . We'll get you cleaned up, and then we can figure out what happened."

I nodded and closed my eyes.

The next hour or so was a blur of cars and sidewalks and hotel hallways, until I finally got my wish and used half the hot water in Chicago in the best shower of my life. I stood there forever, just watching the bloody water spiral down the drain. When I got out, I pulled on the bathrobe hanging on the hook and then wiped the mirror over the sink with a washcloth. I wished I hadn't. I knew I'd have a black eye, but I forgot about the split lip. I looked like I'd been kidnapped, beaten up, and seen my friends die. My head got light and my knees turned to paper, and there I was, on the floor. I wonder how many hours women have logged sitting on bathroom floors. I bet it's a lot. I pulled my hands out of the sleeves of the bathrobe to see what else Margaret got accomplished. Dark red and purple lines, like tattoos around my wrists, one for each zip tie. My hands were still pink, but least they weren't quite so swollen. I could make a fist, not that it would do me any good.

I got to my feet and joined Dr. Bel and Shanti in the sitting area, drinking wine from plastic glasses. I'd never seen Dr. Bel in anything but polished doctor clothes, so to see her with her hair in a ponytail and wearing sweats, was just one more shock. Shanti looked cute as usual in the other hotel bathrobe. My phone, along with most of a pizza and a bottle of orange juice sat on the coffee table.

"We thought you might be hungry," said Dr. Bel.

I laughed. Shanti looked distressed, so I can imagine what it sounded like. "I think it was two days ago, breakfast, so yeah."

.As I ate, I snuck glances at my phone. I didn't want to look at the pictures, but in the end I had to. I scrolled quickly past the video Margaret took, and looked at the pictures March snapped in the forest. I thought he was taking pictures of the trees, but they were all of me; my hair flying around in the breeze, my cheeks pink. I looked happy. I turned it off and set it face down.

Dr. Bel said, "So I checked the ERs for guys with those injuries like I told you I was going to do. Well, a friend of mine at Holy Cross told me a DOA John Doe in black clothes got dumped in their parking lot with what they assumed was a shovel to the head. When you didn't pick up your phone, I had a park ranger check the cabin. When they said no one was there, we went to your house."

"We saw the video," said Shanti. "And we got on the next flight."

"Thank you," I whispered.

"Do you want to talk about what happened?" asked Dr. Bel.

"Marly, my friend is dead," I tried to say it, but I couldn't make a sound other than a cracked whisper.

"Take all the time you need," said Dr. Bel. "We'll be right in the next room." She touched Shanti on the shoulder and they gave me a minute to pull myself together. After a brief conversation between the two of them in the small kitchen, Shanti sat back down and poured me a glass of wine.

"I don't think you have a concussion," said Dr. Bel, "and I think a glass is okay."

"Essential," said Shanti.

"…but if you feel dizzy or your vision gets blurry say something, please."

When I could talk, I told them about the *kitsune*.

"The worst," said Shanti. "I hate those things. Shifty little fuckers."

I wanted to ask about Gaia but that would mean talking about March, and I wasn't ready. Instead, I told them how Margaret had made Marly into a monster, how they put me in the truck, and as much as I could remember about the head statue that turned into a hut. "And there was an old lady. . .really tall…"

"Let's get back to her in a minute," Dr. Bel said, frowning. "Where is March?"

"He's gone."

Her frown deepened. "What do you mean, gone? Where did he go? If he left, how did you. . .Ruby, what is it? What happened?"

I told her how he traded his life for mine, how he acted like deciding to die was some sort of way to take control. She sighed. "A brave and final gesture. He was unique in this world. In any world. His absence makes this a meaner place. He'll be—"

I knew that if I stopped being angry, I'd be sad. I wasn't ready for that, yet. "It was stupid; it was so stupid. He stood there and let her kill him, how is that brave? He could have stayed away and lived—someone would have taken care of him. You would have. He would have been fine. And maybe they would have let me go after a while. Damn him." I smacked the table, and hissed at the pain in my hand. "Why did he come here?"

She reached across the table and gathered my hands in hers, careful not to squeeze them. "It was his decision, and we must honor it. It's not up to you or me to decide whether he did the right thing. To him, it was unbearable that he should try to live as a mortal. Remember what he was, after all." She smiled at me. "But mostly, I think, he did it for you. I'm sure he would agree he was lucky to spend his time as a mortal man with you."

Angry was starting to drain away. I had a feeling sad would be around a lot longer, "How did he even get here?"

"I imagine he watched the video, walked to the highway, and asked someone for a ride." I laughed at that, sort of. "Let's talk about the lady in the hut. What do you remember?"

"She acted nice, like she was doing both of us a favor. But she was just selfish and horrible. She said she wanted March's. . .his heart. So she could be young again. But even if she was young she'd still be awful, with those gross bird feet. . ."

Dr. Bel held her hand up. "Bird feet? You mean, like chicken feet?" I nodded. Scaly, nasty chicken feet. "And she was tall?"

"Like ten feet tall. Barbara Yeager, her name is."

She and Shanti exchanged a look. "No, honey. Her name is Baba Yaga." Her mouth formed a thin line.

"You know her?"

"She's my sister."

13

"**S**he's your what now?"

This was getting crazier by the minute. Suddenly I had a wave of home-sickness. Well, maybe past-sickness is more the right word. I could see myself tending bar with Claudio, and Marly sitting at the bar, and Solange on the stereo, and everything normal. No best friend who dies. No unicorn that turns into a beautiful man who also dies. No doctors you trusted with your secrets who have secrets of their own.

"She's my sister, but I wouldn't say we're close."

I gave a wild laugh. "Thanksgiving is going to be awkward this year." I pushed away from the table. "Tell you what, I'm going to get some sleep and then I'll figure out how to get home. On my own. I'll call Claudio or something. So thanks for everything but I'm out." It was a nice speech but my legs decided not to go along with it and I sat back down hard. Shanti moved the wine glass away and poured me some more juice. Dr. Bel continued as if she hadn't heard me.

"There are many of us, sister deities, but it doesn't mean we have the kind of families you mortals do. We were raised apart, and she is far younger than I am." She lifted her hand when I started to speak. "Yes, she's younger. I know what she looked like. I can easily change my appearance. I thought this one would garner respect among the humans. She doesn't have that gift, but she has others. We all must finally count our days. We have a span much longer than you humans, but limits on our days nonetheless. I didn't know her life was winding down. What she did will serve to restore her span of days—not the near-immortality the horn would have provided, but her clock has been reset. It will also give her the appearance of youth." She shifted uncomfortably. "I think she may have been jealous of her sisters who were more. . .conventional looking. Of me. She may have fixed her face with what she's done, but those feet are forever. I didn't know she was here, or that she was the one who was after March. I don't know that I could have stopped her, but I certainly would have tried."

"Will you go after her?" I asked. "She murdered March. She could have killed me."

Dr. Bel turned to Shanti, who got a glazed look for a minute. "No," Shanti finally said. "There's no one here but us. She's gone. I'm sorry, I can't see where.

"You, too?" Shanti colored and shrugged. "So what do you turn out to be? I guess you can tell if there are any xenos nearby?"

"Yes," she nodded. "It's so I can hunt." Then she smiled at me, her normally soft brown eyes now a blaze of marigold. "Have you ever seen a harpy? Would you like to?"

Dr. Bel put her hand over Shanti's. "I think Ruby's had enough new things for today."

"One more thing,' I said. I had to know. "The *kitsune*. He's the reason we came back early. He said some things and March and I had an argument. Well, I had an argument and March tried to figure out why I was upset."

"Some things?" asked Dr. Bel.

"Who is Gaia?" I asked.

"Now there's a name I've not heard in a while." Dr. Bel toyed with a napkin. "What did the *kitsune* say about her?"

"He made it sound like Gaia was March's long lost love and tried to make me jealous."

"And he succeeded," said Dr. Bel.

"Shifty fucker," Shanti said again. "Well, she was and she wasn't." Dr. Bel raised an eyebrow. "Come on," said Shanti. "You know raptors love to gossip." She made a settling, fluttering motion with her shoulders. "What I heard was that they were sort of like brother and sister."

"Oh, well in that case—"

"And also eternally mated."

"Gross, really?"

Dr. Bel said, "The bonds between them are not like mortals, or even like many elementals."

"They lived in harmony for years without number," said Shanti. "Then things started to change. The world changed, and so did he, or so I heard. He would vanish for years, decades. When he returned to her, their fights would be legendary. Giant trees would fall. Rivers rerouted. The great migratory flocks would fly halfway across the continent to avoid their battles."

"Where did he go?" I asked.

"To live among the humans. She hated it, she hated the humans. She felt it coarsened her world. And finally it was her turn to vanish."

"How long ago was that?"

"I don't know. The story was old when I first heard it. But just because they haven't seen each other in who knows how long doesn't mean he wouldn't go to her if she called for him. Like Dr. Bel said, they're bonded. Does that mean they still loved each other? I can't say."

"Well," I said, "shouldn't we try and find her? To let her know?"

Dr. Bel sighed. "You're a good person to think so, but I'm sure she already knows. Go ahead and get some sleep. We'll fly home tomorrow and get you in front of a doctor who'll look at that eye."

"And what about Marly?"

She sighed. "I honestly don't know what can be done about that."

They dropped me off at my house the next afternoon, once Dr. Bel was satisfied I didn't have a head injury and I was fit to walk myself to and from the car. I have to admit, watching her wrangle a ticket for a beat-up girl with no luggage and no

ID, and then have the three of us upgraded to first class was pretty badass. I think she privately enjoyed having people in her thrall from time to time, after all. I told her I'd come see her for an appointment in a few days, but I needed some time to think and I needed to get back to work. Normal stuff, that was all I wanted.

I unlocked the door and stood very still in the doorway.

Marly was on the couch, asleep. If vamps sleep. The place was the same as when I last saw it, when Margaret and her guys took me. The garlic strands, the mirror, all my special lights were gone. My garlic spray was still in my purse, where I left it two days ago on the other side of the room. Then I realized that the bags I'd left by the door were gone as well—the groceries and our bags and my backpack. And no dishes in the sink. Do vamps tidy up now?

As I watched, trying to decide whether to run, Marly rolled onto her side, and the sunlight slanting between the blinds made a dark and light pattern on her face. The sun was on her face. Nothing happened.

I shut the door, and she yawned and sat up.

"Oh, hey bitch. What time is it? Thank god you're back, it's been a hell of a couple of days. You first, though. Tell me everything. How was he?" She got up, retied my robe and went to the fridge, pulling her hands through her hair. "I'm gonna make some coffee, is that okay?" Then she looked at me again. "Jesus, what happened to you? March didn't do that."

"Marly?" I didn't dare think this could be happening. I was asleep, and dreaming. It was a xeno shape shifter. I really did have a head injury. Or it was a vamp trick.

"Yeah, I must look like ass." She looked at me, concerned. "But at least I don't have a shiner. You win."

I forced myself to come closer. There wasn't any smell. Her eyes were her eyes, maybe a little bloodshot. Her hair was clean. Her fingernails were clean and so were her bare feet. Her throat was smooth. I didn't know how to ask her, so I said, "How are you feeling?"

"Crappy. Hung over. I never had a two-day blackout drunk before, not even in college." She frowned. "Now that I think about it, maybe I wasn't drunk." Her eyes widened. "Maybe I got roofied." She nodded to herself, warming to her story. "Yeah. I ran into that Margaret girl. The virgin." She was watching me carefully, waiting to see how it all fit together; what happened to me, and what happened to her. "She said she was a friend of yours and wanted me to let her into your place. . .I don't remember why. Something to do with March, though. I remember that. We had a beer, I figured I could get some dirt out of her. You were right about her, she's kind of a weirdo. I told her I didn't think it was a good idea but I'd let you know she was looking for you. I finished my beer and got up to leave. . .I think she put something in it, in my beer, because the next thing I know, I'm gross and filthy and sleeping on the hood of your car, out back. March found me."

"What?" I grabbed her wrists. "Are you sure? When?"

"Um, can I have my hands back? What time is it?" She squinted at the clock in the microwave. "Hours ago. It was super early this morning. It was still dark. He woke me up and got me inside, waited until I had a shower, and then he took off. Hey, what's wrong?" She put her arms around me, and I couldn't tell her. I couldn't speak, only cry. She touched my cheek. "Who did this to you? Did you talk to the police? Honey, tell me what happened."

So I told her about Margaret, and how she and the two men broke in, grabbed me and took me to Chicago. I told her about Baba Yaga, and the bargain she made with March. It took a long time to explain why March did what he did, and of course I had to change the ending from 'and then he died' to 'and then I *thought* he died but what really happened was he got transformed back into his own pure and perfect form by his incredibly brave act of selflessness.' What I didn't tell her is what happened to her, and how he brought her back. How his selflessness and bravery saved us both, and how his education saved him, too. I couldn't keep it from her for long, but it would have to wait. "So while I was crying on an airplane because I thought he was dead, he was already back here cleaning your ass up and putting away my groceries."

"Wow." Her eyes were huge. "I was still kind of out of it, but I think he said something about traveling. Are you going to see him again?"

"No, I don't think so," I said, and I felt like it was true. We did what we needed to do, to and for and with each other. The tale of the maiden and the unicorn concluded with maybe not 'happily ever after,' but 'the end.'

"What about Margaret?"

I thought about what Shanti said, about hunting. "I have a few ideas."

14

Another shift at the Hare, and I was bone tired and could hear my bed calling my name. It was late, all the drunks were safely in their beds, and the early joggers weren't up and about yet. A sweet woodsy tang from someone's fireplace hung in the air, and I could see my breath. It was a pretty good night. Marly and her new man dropped by—it's his ex-wife's night with the kid—and everyone tried out the new drinks I've been working on; Campari for bitter, rose liqueur for sweet, prosecco for the spark. Just like life, right? When we closed up, Claudio said he'd lock up and he sent me on my way. I told him to fuck right off, just to let him know I appreciated it. Honestly, I was getting a little tired of the kid-glove treatment. My black eye had faded and the bruises on my face and wrists did, too.

Not everything faded, though.

Dr. Bel and I spent a lot of time figuring out how I

was supposed to feel. I think she had some things to work through, also. She didn't cry when we thought March was dead, but she sure did when we realized he was still alive. I tried to get her to tell me what she'd do about her sister, but she flatly refused to discuss it. I guess it was safer that way. Or maybe she just didn't know.

Of course, she was insistent there wasn't any correct way to process everything that happened, but I wasn't so sure. The way I was doing it couldn't be right; I felt like I was treading water, not moving forward. I just kept seeing him, his eyes closed, light streaming out of him, and the old lady, and the knife. Sometimes I'd still feel grief, only to remember no one was actually dead—except the guy who took a hoof to the head and started the whole thing (and frankly I still thought he had it coming).

You can still grieve when someone is gone, though. They don't have to be dead. Sometimes I could hear March saying he was doing it for me, and I'd feel so guilty I didn't know how to stand it, until I remembered people (and xenos) do things of their own free will. I can only be my own navigator. (That's one of Dr. Bel's, obviously.) And now, of course, I could replace guilt and grief with worry that he'd reappear and Baba Yaga, the old lady who got cheated twice, would come for him again. Or her sister. Or me.

One thing I was crystal clear on, though, was anger. That stayed the same, like a blue flame from a cigarette lighter. I liked to take it out and look at it sometimes. I'm going to show it to Shanti, pretty soon, and maybe we'll go hunting.

But I wasn't thinking about any of that at the moment.

I was all about getting home and misting my orchid and how good it was going to feel to take my bra off, and that's when I smelled roses.

I stopped and looked for the source—not perfume that had roses in it, but real roses, the way they smell at the end of a warm day in spring. Like honey, or apples. And it was pretty easy to see where the sweet fragrance was coming from, because at the side of that late-November street, among the skeleton trees and dried out leaves, a huge rose bush was blooming, tumbling in peach and yellow over a tall garden gate.

The unicorn stood under the roses.

"March." He nodded, or I guess you could say he swung his gorgeous head up and down. "I'm glad you're alive." That sounded stupid. "About Marly. I know you could only do that once. I know you did it for me. I wish I knew how to thank you." He tossed his head, and I could see the silver streak in his hair fell over his eye just the same way as it used to, even though every part of him was different. His nose was plush, perfect charcoal velvet, and I could imagine how soft and warm it would feel under my hand. One second I was wanting to touch him, and the next I was reaching towards him, and he danced backwards, raising a cloud of silver sparks. The roses shivered on their stems, dropping a shower of petals on my hair and jacket. "Oh my god, I'm sorry." I shoved my hands in my pockets. "Look, see? I'd never hurt you. I wasn't thinking." He made a sort of chuffing sound. "I guess you don't want to turn back into a man? Just for a few minutes?" He lowered his head. "Had enough of being person shaped for a while, huh?"

He considered this, and came closer, until I had to squint against the light pouring off of his horn.

"I'm so sorry we argued," I said. "I should have tried harder to understand. Thank you for coming to rescue me. Thank you for a lot of things." He dipped his head, he was so close I could feel his sweet, warm breath, and his horn was like a torch. "I can't stop thinking about you. I've missed you." I closed my eyes.

When the horn touched my cheek, it felt like his hand, alive and gentle. I kept my eyes closed and imagined he really was touching me, running his human hands along the line of my jaw, lightly stroking my lips, and then placing his palm against my neck. Then the light faded and the warmth went with it; I opened my eyes. He was gone.

I raised my own hand to my neck. It was smooth as glass. I took a deep, shuddering breath and the roses rained their sweet scented petals down on me.

I still have my vamp kit under the bed, with the lights and the mirror and whatnot. But I have another bag, just in case. It's got an unopened bottle of bourbon, a CD of Bonnie Raitt's greatest hits, a couple of chocolate bars, a toothbrush, and a map.

Just in case our story has another chapter. Just in case.

Acknowledgements

I wouldn't have even considered this story if The Fabulous Fictionistas hadn't gotten drunk in a cab in Chicago. That was the first time we decided to write as a group. Pure came later, and turned out to be a solo effort, but it started that night. So thank you to Kenya Cooper, Cait Reynolds, Daphne Lamb Griffith, Sami-Jo Cairns and Genevieve Stutz for all the schemes and thanks to whoever bought the first round.

Carly Hayward, the literal Boss of Me, world's greatest editor.

Aurelia Frey of Pretty AF Designs for my glorious cover.

Gladys Gonzales Atwell for scooping me up and covering me with Nerd Girl goodness.

Peter Beagle who was extremely kind to me at a horrible time, and for The Last Unicorn. I hope Amalthea would approve of March.

Also by Kim Alexander

New World Magic:

Pure
The March Effect
The Great Shatter
A Poisoned Garden

The Demon Door:

The Sand Prince
The Heron Prince
The Glass Girl
The River King

About the author

Kim Alexander grew up in the wilds of Long Island, NY and slowly drifted south until she reached Key West. After spending ten rum-soaked years as a DJ in the Keys, she moved to Washington DC, where she lives with two cats, an angry fish, and her extremely patient husband.

Please visit her at kimalexanderonline.com